U0094034

哈福

哈福

外國人怎麼說都聽得懂

好流利！用英語聊不停

我的第一本英語學習書

施孝昌◎著

前言

瞬間學會說流利英語

「學英語好難噢！單字記了又忘，文法規則那麼多，詞類又有變化……；我的英語不好，講錯了很難為情的……」

類似這種不愉快的「共同體驗」，是眾多學英語的人都有的。

Are you one of them?——你也跟他們一樣，有這種挫折感嗎？

If yes,——如果是的話，讓作者告訴你真正問題所在，你會發現，說一口流利的英語其實很簡單，有中學英語程度就夠了。

單字記了又忘確實是很頭疼的事，像作者剛剛問你的：

「你也跟他們一樣，有這種挫折感嗎？」

這句話裡的「挫折感」frustration這個單字就很難記。可是，這句話根本不須要用到frustration嘛。它的正確英語已經寫在前面，就是：

Are you one of them?

這五個英文單字、一個問號，哪個你不認識？

再舉個例子，下班或放學之前，你向同事、同學宣告可以回家了，你想說：

「我今天的工作全都搞定了。」

「搞定」怎麼說？搞定就是「做完」嘛。那「做完」又該怎麼說？本書第二章c單元的「真實會話」，第一句講得清清楚楚：

I am done for the day.

六個英文單字，其中最長的done也不過四個字母。I am done就是「我做完了。」、「我做好了。」、「我都搞定了。」，這句話根本用不上像finished這樣的字眼的。

純正英語的用字是很簡單的，大可不必為了單字難背而煩惱，只要有一本解說很詳盡、例句很淺易、應用面很廣泛的教材，你根本不必擔心文法規則、詞類變化。

就如I am done.是「我做完了」，任何場合你都這麼說，自然、清晰、流利，這就是學英語的重點。

本書都是學英語的重點、都是最純正的美國英語，你可以學到真正美式思考，美式語言表達法，絕不讓你空背無用的中文式、日文式的洋經濱句子。

就像每一本美國AA Bridgers公司所製作的美語教材一樣，你只要跟著MP3配合老師的示範，每學一句話，立刻就在任何場合加以應用，你會學得很快，很有成就。

從今天開始，在自己的腦中，對自己說：學英語是一件快樂的事。每學一句英話，就很高興告訴自己：

Now I can say it!

I am happy.

I am so happy!!

CONTENTS

3. Asking for permission
請求許可的說法

4. Asking for something
要東西的美語

5. Asking for information
蒐集資訊美語

6. Asking for location
旅遊問路美語

8. Ask what to do
要求指導的美語

9. Asking opinion
尋求意見的美語

10. Talking about the past events
用過去式說美語

11. Talking about future plans
與未來有關的美語

12. Getting people to do something
要求別人辦事的美語

13. Talking about something
與事物有關的美語

14. Express feelings
與情緒有關的美語

15. Dealing with moods and feelings
表達感覺的美語

16. During Conversation
會話中的美語

17. Making suggestions and giving advice
提意見的美語

1
Social English
社交場合美語

MP3-2

a inviting

邀請同座

真實會話（在社交場合見面，介紹朋友並且邀請同座…）

M Hi, Mary. I just saw you and your friend sitting over here.
（嗨，瑪麗。我剛好看到妳跟妳的朋友坐在這裡。）

W Oh, yes. This is my friend Roger.
（哦，是的。這是我的朋友羅傑。）

M Glad to meet you, Roger.
（羅傑，很榮幸與你會面。）

Would you two like to share a table with my wife and I?
（你們兩位要不要與我跟我太太同坐一張桌子呢？）

W Thanks for the offer, but we are expecting some other friends.
（謝謝你的邀請，不過我們還在等其他的朋友。）

M O.K. It was good to see you anyway.
（好吧。反正遇見你們覺得很高興。）

W You, too. I'll see you Monday at work.
（遇見你，我們也很高興。星期一上班時再見。）

增強美語實力

為什麼要學習美語？假如不是為了與人溝通、拓展人際關係，根本就不須要辛辛苦苦地學任何外國語。既然學美語是為了增進交往圈，那麼，學習美語也應該從社交場合的美語學起，而不是傳統的 This is a book. 式的學習法。這是有效學習美語應該確立的第一個心理建設！

介紹與自己同行的人給對方認識，不可說 He is...，也不可以說 She is...。不論被介紹的人是男性還是女性，你一定要手心向上，五指併攏，斜指著要被介紹的人說，This is ＋身份＋人名。像上面的「真實會話」裡的 This is my friend Roger.，這句話的 my friend 是身份，Roger 是身份。而身份不欲讓對方知道時，可以省略不說，簡單說 This is Roger. 就行了。

美語是一種很客套的語言，因為它源自英國，央格魯文明是很講究紳士風度的，所以，他們的語言也很講究「客氣」，凡是有人跟你表示好意，願意為你做任何事情，即使你不領情，你還是應該向對方道謝。Thanks for the offer. 的說法雖然明為表示感謝：「謝謝您的好意。」，其實已經是拒絕對方，是「你的好意我心領了。」的意思。

本課的基本句型，我們要學「Would you like to ＋動詞？」的形式。美語中，凡是邀請對方、給對方提建議，問對方要不要做某件事，大概都用 Would you like to 起頭，後面再接要做的動作。例如：「去」的英語是 go，那你問對方「要不要去？」的美語說法就是：Would you like to go? 你這樣記，說流利的美國話就很簡單。自己試驗一下，邀請對方「你要不要跟我一起來？」的美語應怎麼說？（提示：「跟我一起來」的美語是 come with me。）

會話句型進階

Would you like to share a table with my wife and I?
（你們要不要與我和我太太坐在一起？）

» Would you like to sit with us for dinner?
（你們要不要與我們坐在一起用晚餐？）

» Would you like to go for a walk outside?
（你要不要到外面散散步？）

» Would you join me for a drink in the bar?
（你要不要和我一起到酒吧去喝一杯酒？）

加強小會話

M Would you like to share a table with my wife and I?
（你們願不願意與我和我太太坐在一起？）

W Yes. That would be wonderful.
（好的。那樣太好了。）

常用單字成語

glad	[glæd]	高興
share	[ʃɛr]	分享
offer	[ˈɔfɚ]	（邀請、價格…）提議
expecting		期待（expect 現在分詞）
at work		上班時間
go for a walk		散步
join		加入
drink	[drɪŋk]	飲料；酒
bar		酒吧
wonderful	[ˈwʌndɚfəl]	太好了

b Paying
付帳

真實會話（用餐完畢，討論付帳…）

M That was a great meal.
（這一餐飯吃得真好。）

W It was.
（是的，是很好。）

Are we ready to have them bring the check?
（我們可以讓他們拿帳單來了嗎？）

M I think so.
（我想是吧。）

W How do you want to handle the bill?
（你打算怎樣付帳單呢？）

M I had a little more to drink, so we will split the bill in half, and I will get the tip.
（我多喝了一些酒，所以我們把帳單各付一半，然後我來付小費。）

W Sounds fine to me.
（我同意。）

增強美語實力

與朋友一起用餐，我們的習慣是搶著付錢，所以，有時口袋裡沒錢也可以跟朋友一道上餐廳，反正到時候，摸摸口袋、做做樣子，總有別人付錢的，了不起加上一句：「不跟你爭了。」也就老實不客氣，白吃他一頓了。可是，與歐洲國家的人士聚餐時，你就要小心，他們的習慣是各付各的，即使全部消費開在同一張帳單，也要算清楚到底每個人要各付多少錢。你不學會這種美語，那你只好口袋豐滿一些，準備幫大家付錢了。

meal 是「餐飲」，指的是正餐，一般在餐廳指的是午、晚餐。That was a great meal. 表面上說的是「這餐飯吃得夠爽快。」，實際上是暗示：「我吃飽了，該算帳了。」正如前課說過的，美語是一種很客套的語言，掏腰包以前，還是要客套一下。

在中學，你可能學過 check 這個字，課本說它是「支票」的意思，注意：在餐館中，帳單也叫 check，所以你叫餐館的服務員送 check 給你。在國外有的餐館不只收現金，也收支票，在這種情形下，你可以打開支票簿，開一張 check 付帳。

Sounds fine to me. 是純美語說法，意思是「我同意。」，注意：sounds 是加了 s 的。它的原句是 It sounds fine to me.。不過，說話時，It 所指的事大家都明白，在這裡是指付帳的方式，所以把 It 省下了，免得說話不乾不脆，囉哩八唆。

下面「會話句型進階」要學習的，是如何分攤帳單的各種美語說法。handle 原意是「處理」，handle the bill 是如何「處理帳單」，也就是問對方，帳要怎麼分攤的意思。

「加強小會話」裡，The meal is on me. 的 on 是「算在我身上」的意思，也就是說：「我請客！」。如果你嫌如何分攤帳單的美語太麻煩，只要記住 The meal is on me. 這一句也行。當然，你的荷包會因而嚴重受傷。

會話句型進階

How do you want to handle the bill?
（你打算怎麼樣付帳單呢？）

» How should we write this up?
（你要我們如何開帳單？）

» How do you want to get this divided?
（你要怎麼分攤這筆帳？）

» How do you want to divide the cost?
（你打算要如何分攤這筆費用？）

加強小會話

W How do you want to handle the bill?
（你打算要如何付帳單？）

M Don't worry about it.
（不用擔心。）

The meal is on me.
（這頓飯我請客。）

常用單字成語

great	[gret]	太好了
check	[tʃɛk]	帳單
handle	[ˈhændl̩]	處理
a little more		多一些
split	[splɪt]	分開
bill		帳單
split~in half		將～分成二等分
tip		小費
get ~ divided		分攤～
divide	[dɪˈvaɪd]	分開
cost	[kɔst]	花費

MP3-4

C buying dinner 請客

真實會話（用餐完畢，搶著付錢…）

A I really enjoyed my steak!
（我這一份牛排吃得真是愉快！）

B Good. I liked my dinner, too.
（那很好。我也很喜歡我這一份晚餐。）

A Are we ready to go?
（我們可以走了嗎？）

B Yes. Let's get the check.
（可以，我們付帳吧！）

A Why don't you let me get dinner tonight?
（今晚這頓晚餐你何不讓我請客？）

B No, I still owe you from last week.
（不，上個禮拜我還欠你一頓呢。）

增強美語實力

I really enjoy my steak. 基本句型 I enjoy...（我享受了某種東西），有一種很高興、很滿足的感覺。really 是強調「非常」enjoy。

記得上一課所學的 That was a great meal. 嗎？在這裡，你也可以套用那種說法來說，That was a great steak.（這片牛排真好。）記住，學語言要活用。學了就用，進步就快了。

let me get dinner 是指「讓我來付晚餐的錢」，這四個字要連在一起說，最好連 tonight 也一起說，Let me get dinner tonight. 講起來更順口。

Why don't you 從字面上聽起來是一個問句「你何不…？」，好像是想請對方告訴你一個原因，而其實，它所表達的未必是真的想知道原因，很可能只是客氣，不願意把一句話說得太直接而套用這個句型而已。

在社交場合，不徵求同意就幫人付錢，有時會讓對方尷尬，反而得罪對方，所以套上這個 Why don't you let me ... 的說法，在語氣上就婉轉多了。它所表達的還是 Let me...（讓我來吧）或是 Allow me to ...（容許我來吧）的意思。

爭著付錢，有真有假。你若只是故做姿態，可不要做得太過火，弄假成真可就不妙了。見好就收，趕快給對方來一句標準美語，讓他不能反悔。這句話應該怎麼說？簡單得不能再簡單，只要三個字就對了，請看「加強小會話」。

會話句型進階

Why don't you let me get dinner tonight?
（今晚的晚餐你何不讓我請客？）

» Why don't you let me help you carry that?
（讓我來幫你提那個東西吧？）

» Why don't you come over for lunch tomorrow?
（明天你何不到我家來吃午餐？）

» Why don't you call Bill and see if he is coming?
（你何不打個電話給比爾，看他是不是要來？）

加強小會話

A Why don't you let me get dinner tonight?
（今晚的晚餐讓我請客吧。）

B If you like.
（可以啊，如果你想要付帳的話。）

I will get the bill next time.
（下一次我來付帳。）

常用單字成語

enjoy	[ɪnˈdʒɔɪ]	享受
steak	[stek]	牛排
dinner	[ˈdɪnɚ]	晚餐
owe	[o]	虧欠
carry	[ˈkærɪ]	攜帶
come over		到我家來
lunch		午餐
tomorrow	[təˈmɔro]	明天
call	[kɔl]	打電話
next time		下一回

MP3-5

d paying own way
各自付帳

真實會話（用餐完畢，看帳單…）

A I haven't had a meal this good in weeks.
（我好幾個星期都沒有享用過這麼豐盛的食物了。）

B Mine was not as good.
（我的這一份可就沒有那麼好。）

A Has the waiter brought the check?
（服務員把帳單送來了嗎？）

B Yes. Let's take a look at it.
（是的。讓我們來看看帳單吧。）

A Yes. Let's figure out what we each owe.
（好的。我們來算算我們每一個人要付多少錢。）

B I think I probably owe the most.
（我想我大概要付最多吧。）

增強美語實力

Mine was not as good. 的 mine 是「my ＋名詞」。在美語中，要表示「我的某種東西」，而且這個名詞所代表的東西，在先前已經提過，意義已經很明顯，不用再重複時，就用

mine。在這裡，A 說 meal 很好，B 說的也是 meal，所以他不重複說 My meal was not as good.

而說 Mine was not as good. 注意：在中撣文裡 my 和 mine 都翻譯成「我的」，所以很多人會誤用，一定要記住 my 的後面必須有名詞，不能說 My is... 或 My was...。還有，要注意 mine 的發音，亞洲人，特別是中國人，不會發這個字的音，聽起來老是跟 my 沒有分別。請注意聽錄音帶裡示範老師的發音，這是很重要的。

Let's 是 Let us 的縮寫，它表示一種提議，要對方與你共同做一件事情。例如：「去」的美語是 go，所以叫對方「走吧！」或「咱們走吧！」，美語就是 Let's go. 注意 Let's 的後面不能接著用 to，這是一個看似簡單，卻很容易犯的錯。

Let's figure out what we each owe. 這句話有兩個很常用的美語在裡面，一個是 figure out，另一個是 owe。figure out 是「算出結果來」或「想出結果來」。把「算」和「想」用同一個字來表達，是很有意思的語言現象。我們的語言有也這種說法，叫做「盤算」，例如「心裡盤算著划不划算」。美語還有一句很常用的話叫做 I can't figure out.，現在你也應該知道意思了吧？就是「我算不出來。」或是「我不明白。」那麼，另一句也是很常用的說法：I can't figure out why? 你想是什麼意思呢？ owe 的原意是「欠」，美語認為沒有付錢之前的交易，都算負債，所以用 owe 來代表該付的錢。例如：How much do I owe you?（我該付你多少錢？）

會話句型進階

Let's figure out what we each owe.
（讓我們來算算我們每個人要付多少錢。）

» Let's look at the final report.
（讓我們來看看最後的報告。）

» Let's figure out the work schedule for next week.
（讓我們來想想下星期的工作進度吧。）

» Let's work out who will drive tomorrow.
（我們來安排一下明天誰要開車。）

加強小會話

A Let's figure out what we each owe.
（讓我們來算算我們各人要付多少錢。）

B Here, you are better at math than I am.
（給你，你的數學比我好。）

常用單字成語

in weeks		好幾星期
mine	[maɪn]	我的
waiter	[ˈwetɚ]	侍者
brought	[brɔt]	帶來（bring 的過去式）
take a look		看一看
figure out		算一算；想出結果來
probably	[ˈprɑbəblɪ]	或許
the most		最多
final	[ˈfaɪnl̩]	最後的
report	[rɪˈport]	報告
work schedule		工作時間表
drive	[draɪv]	開車
math	[mæθ]	數學

MP3-6

e see you
再見

真實會話 （餐會結束，準備離開…）

A Well, that was a pretty good dinner.
（哎呀，這一頓晚餐真是好。）

B I really liked our waiter.
（我很喜歡我們的服務員。）

A Did we leave him a tip?
（我們有沒有留小費給他？）

B Yes, it's on the table.
（有的，小費放在桌子上。）

A Okay, I guess I will see you Monday morning, then.
（好吧，那麼我想我們星期一早上再見了。）

B Sounds good.
（聽起來是好主意。）

I'll see you later.
（再見了。）

增強美語實力

學美語，一定要學美語思考法。說美語時，想要一邊說再一邊想，照自己的語言直譯是不行的。本課的 see you 和 before it is too late 就是最好的例子。美語的 see you 是指「看見你」，但是加上如 Monday（下星期一）、later（稍後）等意指未來的字，明明時間還沒到，怎麼可能 see you 了呢？可是 See you Monday.、See you later. 卻是最純正、而且天天必用的美語，到底是怎麼回事呢？實際上，它的意思是「再見」，但是你絕不可以因為「再」這個字而加上 again，說成 See you again Monday. 或 See you again later.。美語的思考法是，有 again 就代表不是經常碰面，或是可能一去不回頭，不然就不會強調 again。所以，See you again. 雖然是正確的美語，但暗指著「再會了」，「幾時再見呀」的遺憾、惆悵、與許願，對經常見面的熟人，是不能講的。千萬不要與 See you later. 混淆。

說美語時，經常會在句尾單獨加上 then。一般中學教 then 這個字，大都當成「那時」來說的，可是實際會話上，在一句話的最後說 then，是指「那麼」、「就這樣了」的意思。then 成了一個助詞，有了它語氣就會順得多。不過，要注意 then 在這種用法的發音，由於是一個助詞，它的發音要很輕，不能強過全句主要的概念所在。聽錄音帶裡的示範，跟著學，很容易就學會了。

I guess 也是使用非常頻繁的一句美語，用在句首或單獨在句尾。guess 是「猜」，但 I guess 不是「我猜」，而是表示不很確定，可「是」、可「不是」的感覺。例如有人問起誰願意幫大家去買飲料，你若是很自願的要幫大家跑一趟路，你就很斬釘斷鐵地說：I'll go.（我去！）；假如你四顧一下，沒人吭聲，只好勉為其難承諾去買，這樣的話，美語的說法就是：I guess I'll go.

會話句型進階

Okay, I guess I will see you Monday morning, then.
（好吧，那麼我想我們星期一早上再見了。）

» I guess I should get home before it is too late.
（我想我應該不會太晚回家。）

» I guess we will talk later about the trip to Seoul.
（我想我們稍後還要討論一下到漢城的旅行。）

» I guess we should get out of here before they close the doors.
（我想在他們打烊之前我們得離開了。）

加強小會話

A Okay, I guess I will see you Monday morning, then.
（好吧，那麼我想我們星期一早上再見了。）

B Okay, but if you want to play tennis with me tomorrow, give me a call.
（好，不過假如你明天想要和我一道打網球的話，打個電話給我。）

常用單字成語

pretty	[ˈprɪtɪ]	非常
really	[ˈriəlɪ]	真的
liked	[laɪkt]	喜歡（like 的過去式）
leave	[liv]	留
guess	[gɛs]	猜想
then		那麼
get home		回到家
talk about		談論
later		稍後
play tennis		打網球
give (someone) a call		給（某人）打電話

2
Offering something
善意與服務的美語

MP3-7

a offer a drink

選用飲料

真實會話（有客來訪…）

秘書：Did you find the office okay?
（你找到我們的辦公室沒什麼困難吧？）

來賓：Yes, fine. Thank you.
（是的，還好。謝謝你。）

秘書：Can I get you anything to drink? Coffee, tea, soda, water?
（我可以拿什麼東西請你喝嗎？咖啡、茶、汽水、礦泉水，要哪一樣？）

來賓：I would like some coffee if it is not too much trouble.
（如果不會很麻煩的話，我想要咖啡。）

秘書：It is no trouble at all.
（一點都不麻煩。）

Follow me and I will show you to the visitor area.
（請隨我來，我帶你到來賓室。）

來賓：Thank you. Let me grab my briefcase.
（謝謝你。讓我拿我的手提箱。）

增強美語實力

美國話的 okay 非常好用，除了最常見的表示 Yes，用以回答對方的問話之外，凡是跟「好」、「沒問題」等有關的意念，都可以用 okay 來表達。例如：Are you okay?（你還好吧？），My English test was okay.（我的英文測驗考得還不錯。）等等。所以本課的 Did you find the office okay? 幾乎就是秘書或公司接待員接待首度到訪的來賓時，典型的見面第一句話。要是在家裡接待第一次來訪的客人，稍微改一下，說 Did you find our house okay?（你很順利找到我們家嗎？）就行了。

grab 這個字，若不是英美人士的話，大部份人都不會用。可是在英語世界裡，用得卻非常多。它的意思是「很快地拿」。對於「拿東西」的說法，我們一般只會用 take 來表示，可是 take 表達不出 grab 那種快快「一把抓」的時空感。Let me grab my briefcase. 含有我拿一下手提箱，「很快就來」的意思。本書後幾章還會學到一個非常好用的 grab a bite，到時會解釋。

問客人「你要喝什麼？」，不能說「What do you want to drink?」。雖然直譯時，它好像最接近原句。它的問題出在 what 與 want，英美思考很尊重個人權利，你直接問對方要喝 what，而沒有給對方決定喝與不喝的選擇，是很魯莽的，所以要說 Can I get you anything to drink? 給對方一個說 Yes 或 No 的機會。

會話句型進階

Can I get you anything to drink?
（我可以幫你拿點什麼飲料嗎？）

» Can I do anything to make you comfortable?
（有什麼事情可為你服務，使你感到賓至如歸嗎？）

» Can I bring you something to read while you wait?
（當你等待的時候，要不要我幫你拿什麼東西讓你讀？）

» Can I give you a hand with your bags?
（我可以幫你提你的行李嗎？）

加強小會話

秘書：Can I get you anything to drink?
（要我幫你拿一點飲料嗎？）

來賓：No thanks. I just finished breakfast at the hotel.
（不用了，謝謝。我剛剛才在飯店裡用過早餐。）

常用單字成語

find	[faɪnd]	找到
office	[ˈɔfɪs]	辦公室
soda	[ˈsodə]	汽水
trouble	[ˈtrʌbl̩]	麻煩
no trouble at all		一點也不麻煩
follow	[ˈfɑlo]	跟隨
visitor area		訪客室
grab	[græb]	（口語）拿
briefcase	[ˈbrifˌkes]	手提箱
comfortable	[ˈkʌmfɚtəbl̩]	舒適的
give (someone) a hand		幫（某人）一個忙

MP3-8

b Offer help

主動幫忙

真實會話（朋友無精打采，怎麼回事…）

M You look a little tired.
（你看起來有點累。）

W I am. I have been on the plane for sixteen hours.
（我是有點累。我已經在飛機上待了十六個鐘頭。）

M Is there anything I can do to help?
（有沒有什麼事我可以幫得上忙的？）

W Actually, if you could grab that other suitcase there, it would save a trip back to the car.
（事實上，如果你可以拿那邊的另一個行李箱的話，我就可以省下一趟走到車子的路。）

M No problem!
（沒有問題！）

I can see that you have your hands full.
（我看得出來，你已經騰不出手來了。）

W Thanks. I don't think I would have been able to come back out for the bag.
（謝謝你。我想我累得走不回來提那個行李了。）

增強美語實力

美語很喜歡用「看起來」、「聽起來」這一類的説法，一定要習慣這種句型，説起美國話才會道地。You look a little tired. 裡的 a little 是可以省略的，只説 You look tired. 就可以了，加上 a little 是表示我「覺得」你有一點點累。像這種説對方「累」，並不是很正面的讚美之詞，在美語中總是以較保留的口氣來説，比較客氣。a little 在此的的功能就是這樣。

適時的伸出援手可以結交很多朋友，但不先問就主動幫忙，在亞洲人士來説，可能是古道熱腸，對歐美人而言，卻是多管閒事。在這種歐美思維方式底下，要幫忙不能直接就「來來來，讓我來。」，一定要説：Is there anything I can do to help?（有沒有幫得上忙之處？）。簡單一點可以説：Is there anything I can do? 本書稍後會學到 If there is anything I can do, let me know.（若有什麼幫得上忙得地方，就告訴我。）也是非常慣用的説法。

在「加強小會話」中，有人主動表示善意要幫忙，假如不需要幫忙，可以説：Not really.。它的意思就是 No.。但是在凡事都要講究「政治正確」（politically correct）的今天，對別人的善意少説 No.，多用 Not really. 絕對是沒錯的。

會話句型進階

Is there anything I can do to help?
（有沒有我可以幫得上忙的地方呢？）

» Is there anything left out in the car?
（有沒有什麼東西留在車上呢？）

» Is there anyone who can help you with your problem?
（有沒有人可以幫你解決你的問題呢？）

» Is anyone helping you with your report?
（有沒有人已經在幫你做報告了呢？）

加強小會話

M Is there anything I can do to help?
（有沒有什麼可以幫得上忙的地方？）

W Not really.
（沒有吧。）

I got everything taken care of earlier this morning.
（我今天早上稍早的時候，已經把所有東西打點妥當了。）

常用單字成語

a little		有一些
look tired		看起來很累
plane	[plen]	飛機
actually	[ˈæktʃʊəlɪ]	實際上
suitcase	[ˈsutˌkes]	行李箱
save a trip		省下一趟路
problem	[ˈprɑbləm]	問題
have (someone's) hands full		（某人的）兩手都拿滿東西
bag	[bæg]	行李
left out		遺留
got everything taken care of		所有事物都打點好了

MP3-9

C offer transportation
搭便車

真實會話（朋友汽車壞了…）

W Well, I am done for the day.
（喏，我今天的工作都做完了。）

How about you?
（你呢？）

M Actually, my car is in the shop, so I have to wait until my wife gets off work later tonight.
（事實上，我的車子進廠送修了，所以今天晚上我必須要等到稍後我太太下班才能走。）

W I can give you a lift home if you like.
（如果你願意的話，我可以送你一程。）

M Are you sure it wouldn't be any trouble?
（你確定那不會麻煩嗎？）

W None at all.
（一點都不麻煩。）

Let's go.
（我們走吧。）

M O.K. Let me just call my wife to let her know.
（好吧。讓我給我太太打個電話，讓她曉得。）

會話句型進階

I can give you a lift home if you like.
（如果你願意的話，我可以送你一程。）

» I can bring you to work in the morning.
（明天早上我可以載你來上班。）

» I can drop your stuff off if you need me to.
（如果你要幫忙，我可以順道把你的東西帶過去。）

» I can write the report if need be.
（如果有報告需要寫的話，我可以寫。）

增強美語實力

搭便車或順道用汽車送朋友一程，在美語會話中是經常碰到的話題。英文裡的說法很多，純美語的說法是give 某人a lift。lift的原意是「舉起來」，從這個意思衍伸的用法很多，既可表示動作，也可表示事務，所以很好用。give a lift是把人「載」上汽車來，所以，I can give you a lift.就是「我可以載你。」，若是有前往的目的地，直接加在句後就行。例如：I can give you a lift home.（我可以載你回家。）或I can give you a lift to work.（我可以載你去上班。）

中學裡應該都學過「早晨」的說法是in the morning.，並不專指哪一天的早晨，例如：six o'clock in the morning（早晨六點）。但美國話in the morning可以指「明天早上」，也就是tomorrow morning的意思。例如：I'll do it in the morning.（我明天早上才做。）分辨的方法是：說話時帶有will、shall等表示未來的字，包括縮寫的說法I'll，則in the morning是指明天早上。此外，要是說話的時間是在下午以後，並且談到in the morning時，卻不用過去式動詞，也是指隔天早上而言。

美語有一個字 stuff，也特別好用，它泛指一切事物，例如：your stuff 指「你的東西」，good stuff 指「好東西」，bad stuff 是「有不良影響的東西」。所以，香菸是 bad stuff，水果對你的健康是 good stuff。測驗一下，Bring your stuff with you. 是什麼意思？對了，就是提醒對方「帶著你的東西。」

加強小會話

M I can give you a lift home if you like.
（如果你願意的話，我可以用車載你回家。）

W No, thanks.
（不，謝謝你。）
I actually have a lot of work to catch up on.
（我實際上還有很多工作必須要趕工。）

常用單字成語

in the shop		進廠送修
get off work		下班
give (someone) a lift		（口語）開車送某人
sure	[ʃʊr]	確定
none	[nʌn]	一點也沒有
morning	[ˈmɔrnɪŋ]	早晨
drop	[drɑp]	掉
drop~off		卸（貨）
stuff	[stʌf]	（口語）物品
catch up		趕上

MP3-10

d offer food

吃點東西吧！

真實會話（親友遠途開車來訪…）

A Did you have a good drive in?
（你開車到這裡來，一路還好吧？）

B Yes, but it was a little longer than I expected.
（還好，不過比我預期的還要久一些。）

A Did you stop along the way?
（你路上有停留嗎？）

B No. I drove straight through.
（不。我直接開到這兒來的。）

A You must be hungry!
（你一定很餓了！）

Please, let me get you something to eat.
（無論如何，都得讓我幫你弄點吃的，不要推辭。）

B That would be great.
（那太好了。）

I'm starving!
（我真的太餓了！）

增強美語實力

還記得 Did you find our house okay? 嗎？要是不記得，請翻回前幾課溫習一下。這裡的情況與那一課有點類似，都是有訪客到來。但這回是開車來訪，也未必是首度到訪，所以才問對方 Did you have a good drive in?。注意這裡的 in，它不是普通常見的「在裡面」的意思，在這裡它是指「到來」。例如：The train is not in yet.（火車還沒來。）

小心 You must be hungry. 的用法，這裡的 must 不是「必須」，像是 We must go now.（我們現在一定得走了。）的用法。You must be... 講的是「你必定……」，也就是帶有點猜測的含意。例如：You must be Jane's mother.（妳必定是珍恩的媽媽吧？）我們學過「很累」的美語是 tired，所以「你必定累了。」的美語該怎麼說？

第一章中，我們學到 why don't you 的用法，也解釋過 let me 的用法，這裡我們要再練習一下這個用法。Let me get you something to eat. 是對熟人說的，對較陌生的人，應該更客氣一點用 Can I... ？的句型。還記得前面說過 Can I get you anything to drink? 的用法嗎？

即使是熟人，講話還是不能不客氣，所以明明主動要拿東西給人吃，說的是 Let me get you something to eat.，心裡想的是「別推辭了」，但口頭上還是加了 please（求你）。亞洲人看起來，覺得很奇怪，拿東西請人吃，幹嘛求人家？不過說美國話，加了 please 才算盡了主人的心意。欲說一口流利道地的美語，這是不能不注意的。

會話句型進階

Please, let me get you something to eat.
（請你別客氣，讓我幫你弄點吃的。）

» Let me help you with those bags.
（讓我幫你提那些行李。）

» Let me give you a hand with that box.
（讓我幫你拿那一個盒子。）

» Let me find something for you to write with.
（讓我幫你找樣東西，給你用來寫字。）

加強小會話

A Please, let me get you something to eat.
（請你別客氣，讓我幫你弄點吃的。）

B No, thanks. I brought a sandwich with me in the car.
（不用了，謝謝。我自己帶有三明治放在車上。）

常用單字成語

along	[ə'lɔŋ]	沿著
straight	[stret]	直的
through	[θru]	穿越
straight through		直接到底；不曾停留
must be		必定是
hungry	['hʌŋgrɪ]	餓
starving	['stɑrvɪŋ]	很餓
sandwich	['sændwɪtʃ]	三明治

MP3-11

e offer to lend something
借東西

真實會話（要工作，卻少了工具…）

A I am trying to put this shelf together, but I don't have the right tools.
（我想要把這個架子組合起來，但是我沒有正確的工具。）

B What do you need?
（你需要什麼工具呢？）

A I need a socket set.
（我需要一組扳手的套筒。）

I had one, but I lent it to my son.
（我有一套，可是我借給我兒子了。）

B You are welcome to borrow my set if you want.
（如果你需要的話，很歡迎你借我的。）

A Really? That would make this a lot easier.
（真的嗎？那我的工作就簡單多了。）

B No problem.
（沒有問題的。）

I will go get them.
（我去把它們拿來。）

增強美語實力

美語 a set 是指「一套」。在 a 與 set 之間加上名詞，就是特指成套的某種東西，例如：a socket set 是五金工具裡的一套扳手套筒，而 a tool set 就是一整套包括螺絲起子、小扳手等等的工具。

請注意 lent to my son 和 borrow my set 的用法。lent 是 lend 的過去式型態，而 lend 和 borrow 都是「借」的意思。不過 lend 是「借出去」，borrow 是「借進來」，所以對我來說是 I lent you my set.，對你而言，你是 borrowed my set. 由此可見，我們上圖書館是去 borrow books；我的車壞了，要向你 borrow your car。

You are welcome. 單獨成句時，很多人應該都會說，就是用來回答 Thank you. 的話，表示「不用客氣」。若要告訴對方，他要做什麼事，儘管去做，不必客氣，也可用 You are welcome 起頭，記得加上 to 就可以。例如「跟我們在一塊」的美語是 be with us，則「歡迎你同我們在一起」或「別客氣，儘管與我們在一起」的說法就是 You are welcome to be with us.

I will go get them. 是純美語的用法。go 是動詞，get 也是動詞，兩個動詞竟然連在一起用，有的中學英文老師會皺眉頭！不過要是有人說 I will go to get them.，筆者卻要大大地皺眉頭！好幾億以英、美語為母語的人士也會皺眉頭噢。學美語不能死抱八十年前的文法規則，要記住語言是活的，所以 go 的後面直接加動詞，是正確的，而且一定要這樣講，美語才純正。看看這些例子：go see a movie（去看電影）；go get a sandwich（去買個三明治）；go borrow a book（去借書）。好了，你知道「去找點東西吃」的美語怎麼說嗎？提示：還記得 get something to eat 嗎？

會話句型進階

You are welcome to borrow my set if you want.
（如果你需要的話，很歡迎你借我那一套。）

» You are welcome to come by for dinner tonight.
（今天晚上很歡迎你過來吃晚餐。）

» You are welcome to ride with us to the store.
（我們很歡迎你跟我們一起搭車去商店。）

» You are more than welcome to join the club.
（我們非常歡迎你加入這個俱樂部。）

加強小會話

A You are welcome to borrow my set if you want.
（如果你要的話，很歡迎你借我的那一套。）

B No, thanks. I need to get a new set anyway.
（不，謝謝你。反正我自己需要買一套新的。）

常用單字成語

shelf	[ʃɛlf]	架子
put~together		組合（某物）
right	[raɪt]	正確的
tool	[tul]	工具
socket	[ˈsɑkɪt]	（扳手的）套筒
a set		一套
borrow	[ˈbɑro]	借
easier	[ˈizɪɚ]	比較簡單
ride	[raɪd]	乘車
store	[stor]	商店
club	[klʌb]	俱樂部

3

asking for permission

請求許可的說法

MP3-12

a from boss

要求請假

真實會話（職員找主管談話…）

職員：Excuse me, do you have a minute?
（對不起，你有時間嗎？）

主管：Sure, Mike.
（麥可，當然有。）

What do you need?
（你有事嗎？）

職員：Could I get Friday off to take my kids to the zoo?
（星期五我可以請假帶我的小孩到動物園嗎？）

主管：Are you caught up on your project?
（你那個專案進度都沒有問題嗎？）

職員：Yes, I will finish writing summary today.
（是的，我今天可以把整個綜合摘要寫完。）

主管：That's fine, then.
（那好吧。）

Just ask me ahead of time in the future.
（不過，以後要提早問我一下。）

增強美語實力

當有人向你說 Excuse me, do you have a minute? 就是有事要找你了。Excuse me 雖然有「對不起」的意思，但那是想引起你的注意，不是道歉。Do you have a minute? 才是主題，但也不是真正要看看你有沒有時間，而是「我有事找你談」的另外一種說法。

注意 Could I get Friday off? 的說法。星期五要請假，那星期五應該還沒到，怎麼會用過去式 could ？這種美語用法很普遍，一般是表示尊敬對方。對很熟的人，或對下輩可以不用過去式，用 Can、May 就可以。

還記得 then 在句尾的用法嗎？ That's fine, then. 又是一個好例子。

英語有些字，後面所接的字有一定的格式，不能隨便。finish（完成）就是一例，它的後面要是接一個動作，一定要用 ing 形式，文法上稱為接動名詞。如：finish working（把工作做完），finish smoking（把香菸抽完），finish writing（把寫作做完）。

「加強小會話」裡，主管不准假，他的理由是 on such short notice，意思是「通知太晚」。注意這裡用 short（很短），不是 notice 的長短，而是時間太短。

商務美語會用到一些商務上常用的字，例如本課的 proposal（企畫），project（專案）等等，單字有點長，發音有點麻煩，但既然出現在本書，必屬最、最、最常用字，一定要記。跟者錄音帶老師的示範，會記得比較快，而且發音會很自然，用起來當然會得心應手。

會話句型進階

Could I get Friday off to take my kids to the zoo?

（我星期五可以請假帶我小孩上動物園嗎？）

» Could I borrow your pen for a minute?
（我可以借用你的筆一會兒嗎？）

» Could I have Mark help me write the proposal?
（我可以請馬克幫我寫這一個企畫嗎？）

» Could I get you to proofread my report?
（我可以請你幫我校閱一下我的報告嗎？）

加強小會話

職員：Could I get Friday off to take my kids to the zoo?
（我星期五可以請假帶我小孩上動物園嗎？）

主管：I am sorry, but I cannot let you go on such short notice.
（對不起，你這麼晚通知我，我不能讓你走。）

常用單字成語

minute	[ˈmɪnɪt]	（時間）分
have a minute		（口語）有時間
get (time) off		請假
kid		（口語）小孩
project	[ˈprɑdʒɛkt]	專案
finish	[ˈfɪnɪʃ]	完成
summary	[ˈsʌmərɪ]	綱要
ahead of time		提早
in the future		未來
proposal	[prəˈpozḷ]	企畫
proofread	[ˈprufˌrid]	校閱
notice	[ˈnotɪs]	通知

MP3-13

b from host
宴會上

真實會話（徵求主人同意…）

主人： I hope everyone is enjoying the party.
（我希望這個宴會上，每個人都玩得很愉快。）

來賓： I know my wife and I are.
（我知道我跟我太太都很愉快。）

主人： Good. We are about ready for dinner.
（好極了。我們即將準備好用晚餐。）

來賓： Would it be okay for me to make a toast tonight?
（今天晚上由我來祝酒可以嗎？）

主人： That would be fine.
（那沒有問題。）

What do you want to toast?
（你打算慶祝什麼呢？）

來賓： It is a surprise.
（那可是個秘密。）

增強美語實力

本課我們來探討「英語」或「美語」學習法。

學習外國語言，經常聽到「句型」這個名詞。到底什麼叫做句型？在實際會話上，句型就是「用固定的幾個字作為說話的起頭或結尾」，並在句子其他適當的地方，將你要表達的意思講出來。如：I hope everyone is enjoying the party. 的句子中，主要的意思是 everyone is enjoying the party.（每個人在宴會上都很愉快）。你要是把 everyone 的第一個字母用大寫字來寫，句子就成為 Everyone is enjoying the party.，你看，它就很像學校英文課本裡的句子了，不是嗎？但是，實際講話時，你不可以講得像背書一樣呆板，人是有七情六慾的，你還必須表達自己的一些感覺、情緒、願望、判斷等等，這些就要靠著「固定的幾個字」來起頭或結尾，也就是需要某種句型來表達。以句型來說，I hope 這兩個字永遠出現在句首，是「我期待」，「但願」的意思。只要你心裡有這種「願望」的念頭，就順口溜出 I hope，然後把真正願望的事簡單說出來，你的美語就會顯得很流利又自然。例如「我真希望你快樂」的美語說法：先說 I hope，然後「你快樂」美語說法是 you are happy，照著講整句話就是 I hope you are happy.

按照這種「固定句型＋想法」的方法學美語，學起來既不枯燥，又很快、很有效！

surprise 一般譯做「驚奇」，但講話中不會用「驚奇」這種字眼，所以你要記得它的意思是「出乎意料之外」，凡是任何可以讓人覺得意外的，都可以用 surprise 這個字。在本課對話中，It is a surprise. 指的是要「讓大家到時覺得很意外」，所以是「那是個秘密」的意思。很多人都單靠一本英漢字典，或英和字典、英韓字典等學英語，一想到「秘密」，就想到 secret，這樣英語是永遠學不好的，一定要有一本很實際的書，很詳盡的解說，活學活用才行。

會話句型進階

Would it be okay for me to make a toast tonight?
（今天晚上由我來祝酒可以嗎？）

» Would it be all right if we left early?
（如果我們早一點離開可以嗎？）

» Would it be all right to invite the Smiths?
（邀請史密斯一家人可以嗎？）

» Would it be okay with you if I brought my kids?
（如果我帶我的小孩來，會給您造成什麼問題嗎？）

加強小會話

來賓：Would it be okay for me to make a toast tonight?
（今天晚上由我來祝酒可以嗎？）

主人： I would rather you did it after dinner.
（我寧願你等到晚餐過後再祝酒。）

常用單字成語

hope		希望
party	['pɑrtɪ]	宴會
about		大約
make a toast		祝酒
surprise	[sɚ'praɪz]	秘密；驚奇
all right		沒問題
early	['ɝlɪ]	早
invite	[ɪn'vaɪt]	邀請
would rather		寧願

MP3-14

C from guest 用 Do you mind 尋求許可

真實會話（體貼的主人準備介紹新來賓…）

主人：Did you find the place all right?
（你找到這個地方沒有問題吧？）

來賓：Yes, I did.
（是的，沒有問題。）

主人：Good. Do you mind if I take you around and introduce you to everyone?
（很好。我帶你四處走走，把你介紹給每位來賓，你介意嗎？）

來賓：No, that would be nice.
（不，那樣很好。）

主人：I know it can be tough to mingle when you don't know anyone.
（我知道，你不認識任何人的話，要融入一群人是很困難的。）

來賓：Yes, I have only been in town for four days now.
（是的，我到本市來才不過幾天的功夫。）

增強美語實力

希望從前面幾課你已經學會 Did you find the place all right? 的用法。all right 是 fine, okay 的意思，所以這句話跟前面 Did you find the office okay? 用法是一樣的。

我們學過 Could I take Friday off? 的句型，在那裡是用 Could I? 來尋求對方的同意。我們也學過 Please, let me get you something to eat. 這種用「請你讓我來……」的句型，本課我們來學一個 Do you mind...? 的句型。我們說 Do you mind...? 是個「句型」，因為它永遠出現在句首，含意是「假如我這樣做，你會介意嗎？」，也就是「你讓不讓我這樣做？」的意思。至於想做的事，有兩種表達方式，一種是用 if（假如），另一種是簡單用動名詞就行（還記得什麼叫做動名詞？記得前面說過 finish writing，finish working 嗎？）。例如「我在這裡抽煙」的美語是 I smoke here，於是問對方「在這裡抽煙行不行？」的美語就是 Do you mind if I smoke here? 或 Do you mind my smoking here?。很簡單，不是嗎？試試看，「我把東西留在這裡」的美語是 I leave my stuff here，那問對方「可不可以把東西留在這裡」怎麼說？

會話句型進階

Do you mind if I take you around and introduce you to everyone?
（如果我帶你四處逛逛，把你介紹給每個人，介意嗎？）

» Do you mind my asking about your family?
（你介意我問你有關你家庭狀況嗎？）

» Do you mind if I take your coat?
（請把外套脫下來好嗎？）

» Do you mind if I smoke?
（我抽煙，你介意嗎？）

加強小會話

主人：Do you mind if I take you around and introduce you to everyone?
（我帶你四處逛逛，把你介紹給每一個人，你介意嗎？）

來賓：Actually, Sally already offered to take me around.
（事實上，莎莉已經答應要帶我四處逛。）

Thanks, though.
（不過，還是很謝謝你。）

常用單字成語

mind	[maɪnd]	介意
introduce	[ˌɪntrəˈdjus]	介紹
nice	[naɪs]	很好
tough	[tʌf]	（口語）困難
mingle	[ˈmɪŋgḷ]	打成一片
in town		在本地
family	[ˈfæməlɪ]	家人
coat		外套
smoke		抽煙
already	[ɔlˈrɛdɪ]	已經
though	[ðo]	（口語）還是

MP3-15

d from group
臨時改變決定

真實會話（時間已遲，該來的人還沒來…）

A I wonder where Mr. Huang is.
（我在想，黃先生到底在哪裡？）

B I don't know.
（我不知道。）

He was supposed to chair the meeting.
（他應該是要主持這項會議的。）

A Does anyone care if I go ahead and open the meeting until Mr. Huang gets here?
（如果我逕行主持開會，直到黃先生抵達，有人介意嗎？）

B No, we need to get going.
（不，我們得開始了。）

A Okay, then. Everyone please be seated.
（那好吧。請各位就座。）

B We are ready when you are.
（我們都準備好了，你隨時可以開始。）

增強美語實力

I wonder是一個很常用的美語句型，也是永遠出現在句首，意思是「我在想」、「我在猜」、或「我好納悶」，也就是心裡有疑問，搞不懂。它有兩種用法，一種是接if，下一課會說明；另一種是接who、where、when、what、how等表示疑問的字。注意：在疑問詞後面的字，順序有異常，很多人在這裡犯了錯。「他在哪裡」的美語原本是Where is he? 可是「我好納悶他到底在哪裡？」的美語是I wonder where he is.。注意is的位置。如果你對文法術語好奇，這種從疑問句is he? 的形式變成he is. 的肯定句形式，在文法上叫做「間接問句」。請問：「我心裡在想她到底是誰？」美語怎麼說？提示：「她是誰？」的美語是Who is she?

本課延續上一課Do you mind...? 的句型，介紹另一個非常好用的美語單字care。care的意思很多，基本上都含有「關心」的意味。mind是「介意」，care是「關心」、「在乎」，所以這兩個字，在這裡是可以互換的。Do you mind if...? 就是Do you care if...? 不過，要注意，Do you mind可以接動名詞，但Do you care不接動名詞，因為接動名詞會有句子缺字的感覺。例如：可以說Do you mind if I leave my stuff here?（你介意我把東西留在這裡嗎？），也可說Do you care if I leave my stuff here?。你可以說Do you mind my smoking here?（你介意我在這裡抽煙嗎？），但不要用Do you care my smoking的說法。

open the meeting是宣佈開始開會，這是一句正確的美語，open是「開」的意思，很多中國人除了open the door（開門），open the window（開窗）以外，像open the game（開賽）、open the meeting（開會）這種道地的美語就不會講，反倒把open拿來講「開燈」，「開收音機」。我們絕不要犯這個錯，講「開燈」這種打開電器開關的「開」，不能用open，要用turn on。

會話句型進階

Does anyone care if I go ahead and open the meeting until Mr. Huang gets here?
（如果我就這樣先主持會議，直到黃先生到來，各位介意嗎？）

» Do any of you mind if I leave early?
（如果我提早離開，你們當中有人介意嗎？）

» Does anyone mind if I eat my lunch here?
（如果我在這裡吃午餐的話，有人介意嗎？）

» Does anyone mind if I take this chair?
（我把這張椅子搬過來坐，有人介意嗎？）

加強小會話

A Does anyone care if I go ahead and open the meeting until Mr. Huang gets herc?
（如果我逕行開始主持會議，直到黃先生到來，各位介意嗎？）

B We should probably let Bob do it.
（我們或許應該讓鮑伯來主持。）

He is the co-chair of the committee.
（他是委員會的共同主席。）

常用單字成語

wonder	[ˈwʌdɚ]	猜想
supposed	[səˈpozd]	（口語）應該
chair		主持；椅子
chair the meeting		主持會議

care	[kɛr]	在意
go ahead		逕行
get going		進行
please	[pliz]	請
be seated		坐下
get here		抵達
committee	[kəˈmɪtɪ]	委員會

e permission from co-worker
借東西

真實會話（John 的電腦壞了…）

A Good morning, Sally.
（莎莉，您早。）

B Morning, John.
（約翰，您早。）

What can I do for you?
（有什麼事可以幫你做嗎？）

A I was wondering if I could borrow your laptop.
（我在想是否可以借妳的膝上型電腦。）

My computer is down today.
（我的電腦今天壞了。）

B I need my laptop for a meeting this afternoon, but you can sit at my desk and use my computer.
（我今天下午開會需要我的膝上型電腦，不過你可以坐在我的辦公位置用我的桌上型電腦。）

A Are you sure I won't be in your way?
（妳確定我不會妨礙妳的工作嗎？）

B I'm sure.

（我很確定。）

I will be in the project room all morning.

（我整個早上都會待在專案室裡。）

增強美語實力

相信大家都會 Good morning.（早安）這句話。但怎麼回答人家對你問早呢？你可以回答 Good morning.，但是要注意說話的調子跟第一個道早的人不同，先道早安的人，說的調子是 good morning，重音在 mor，回答的人說 good morning，重音在 good。對很熟的人，有一個不用去管語調的回答法，直接說 Morning. 就可以了。但是，這樣的說法，有一種稱兄道弟的隨便感覺，若不是對很熟的鄉親朋友，還是要回答 Good morning 的好。

I was wondering 與 I wonder 的說法略有不同，表達的心裡感覺也略有不同，I was wondering 有強調「一直」在想的含意。不過兩者的用法是一樣的，它們的後面接 if，用來表示「我在想是否……」。下面「會話句型進階」中有更多的例子。

美語的 down 原意是「向下面」，很多反面不愉快的事，都可以用 down 來表示。電腦壞了是 down，人的心情不佳也是 down。

laptop 是電腦用語，指的是可攜帶型的電腦，它是相對於桌上型的 desktop 所創出來的字。lap 是人膝上大腿部的地方，可攜行的電腦大多靠在這個部位操作，所以稱為 laptop。近來 laptop 的體積越來越小，很像筆記簿，所以 notebook 的說法有取代 laptop 的趨勢。

會話句型進階

I was wondering if I could borrow your laptop.
（我在想，我是否可以借你的膝上型電腦？）

» I was wondering if I could use your desk this morning.
（我在想，今天早上是否可以用你的辦公桌？）

» I was wondering if I could use your phone .
（我在想，我是否能使用你的電話？）

» I was wondering if I need to let you know before I leave for the day.
（我在想，今天我離開之前是否要先讓你知道？）

3. asking for permission

加強小會話

A I was wondering if I could borrow your laptop.
（我在想，我是否可以借你的膝上型電腦？）

My computer is down today.
（今天我的電腦壞了。）

B Sure. Just get it back to me tomorrow morning.
（當然可以。只要在明天早上把它還給我就行。）

常用單字成語

laptop	[ˈlæpˌtɑp]	膝上型電腦
computer	[kəmˈpjutɚ]	電腦

down		（口語）故障了
afternoon	[ˌæftɚˈnun]	下午
in (someone's) way		妨礙（某人）
phone	[fon]	電話
leave	[liv]	離開
leave for the day		下班
get ~ back		把（某物）送回

4

asking for something

要東西的美語

MP3-17

a in the plane

在飛行途中

真實會話（搭機旅行途中…）

空姐：Did you press the call button?
（您按了呼叫服務的按鈕嗎？）

旅客：Yes, I did.
（是的，我按了。）

空姐：What can I do for you?
（有什麼事可以幫您服務呢？）

旅客：Can I get a glass of water to take my aspirin?
（我要吃我的阿斯比靈，可以跟妳要一杯水嗎？）

空姐：Sure! Would you like ice with that?
（沒有問題！你要不要加冰塊？）

旅客：No, thank you.
（不用了，謝謝妳。）

增強美語實力

美語的 call 有很多種含意，在日常會話中最常用的意思是「叫人」、「打電話」、和「拜訪」。這裡的 call button 是飛機上用來呼叫空中小姐服務的按鈕。

吃藥的動作，在美語一定要用 take 這個字，不能用 eat，就像是中文裡吃藥可以説成「服藥」，但吃飯不能説成「服飯」一樣的道理，take aspirin、take a pill（吃藥丸）這種字最好當成一個詞來記。

a glass of 是「一杯」的意思。這裡的 glass 原指玻璃杯，但習慣上 a glass of 已經成為計算飲料的單位，所以跟 a cup of（一杯）用法有時可以相通。例如 a cup of water、a glass of water。但要注意，像咖啡、可可等在歐美是喝熱的，不用玻璃杯裝，所以只能用 a cup of coffee 來敘述。縱使在亞洲，你喝的是冰咖啡，盛在玻璃杯裡面，但 a glass of coffee 還是很奇怪的，不要這樣説。

會話句型進階

Can I get a glass of water to take my aspirin?
（可以跟你要一杯水，來吃我的阿斯比靈嗎？）

» Can we get up from our seats yet?
（我們可以離開座位了沒有？）

» Can I get a movie to watch?
（我可以借一部電影來看嗎？）

» Can I get a pillow and a blanket?
（我可以要一個枕頭和一條毯子嗎？）

加強小會話

旅客：Can I get a glass of water to take my aspirin?
（我要吃我的阿斯比靈，可以跟妳要一杯水嗎？）

空姐：Yes, but it will be a few minutes.
（可以，不過要等幾分鐘。）

常用單字成語

press	[prɛs]	按下
button	[ˈbʌtn̩]	按鈕
call button		（飛機上）叫服務的按鈕
glass		玻璃杯
aspirin	[ˈæspərɪn]	（藥）阿斯比靈
ice	[aɪs]	冰
get up		起身
watch		看
pillow	[ˈpɪlo]	枕頭
blanket	[ˈblæŋkɪt]	毯子
a few		幾個

MP3-18

b in the hotel
投宿飯店

真實會話（在飯店中，怕睡過頭…）

旅客：Hello, is this the front desk?
（喂，這是服務台嗎？）

服務員：Yes, it is.
（是的。）

旅客：This is Jimmy Huang in room 512.
（我是五一二號房的黃吉米。）

服務員：What can I do for you, Mr. Huang?
（黃先生，有什麼可以為您服務的呢？）

旅客：I was wondering if I could get a five-thirty A.M. wake up call.
（我想是否可以請您明天早上五點半叫我起床。）

服務員：Yes. I will see to it.
（好的。我會負責辦到。）

增強美語實力

打電話時，不論是撥電話的人或是接電話的人，開頭第一句一定是先表明身份。而美國話表明或詢問身份一定用 this，不能用 I、you。例如：告訴對方「我是老王」，要說：This is

Wang.；問對方是誰，要說：Who is this?

飯店中，一般有定時叫醒旅客的「晨呼」服務，稱為 morning call 或 wake up call。

I will see to it 看起來很簡單，也真的是最常用的美語之一，但很多人學了很多年美語、英語，不但不會用，連聽都聽不懂。see 當然是指「看」，含意是沒變的，但注意它在這裡不是指「看見東西」see it，而是 see to it，有個 to 表示「看顧」的對象，所以 I will see to it. 真正的意思是「我會看著它發生」，亦即「我會落實處理這件事」學習美語，最好是常用的字多學一些，不常用的字，不要浪費時間去記。多用常用字，可以使你用字活潑，例如，在會話中，答應對方的要求，或同意對方的看法，不能靠一個 yes 打通關，東一個 yes，西一個 yes，令人覺得與你談話非常乏味，你可以稍加變化：True.（沒錯。）、Sure.（當然。）、All right.（好！）等等都很好用。「加強小會話」中，有 absolutely 這個字，字雖然長一些，但很常用，表示「絕對沒問題！」，強調絕對不會出差錯，在服務業，回答客戶 Absolutely. 比回答 Yes. 好多了，所以務必要學。

會話句型進階

I was wondering if I could get a five-thirty A.M. wake up call.
（我在想，是否可以請你明天早上五點半叫我起床？）

» I was wondering if I could have a menu brought to my room.
（我在想，是否可以請你把菜單送到我的房間來？）

» I was wondering if there was a place to eat nearby.
（我在想，附近是否有地方可以用餐？）

» I was wondering if you could have the maid sent up to clean my room.
（我在想，你們是不是能派一個女清潔工上來清理我的房間？）

加強小會話

旅客：I was wondering if I could get a five-thirty A.M. wake up call.
（我在想是否可以請你們明天早上五點三十分叫我起床。）

服務員：Absolutely.
（絕對沒有問題。）

Would you like us to call again later as well?
（你要我們稍後再叫你一次嗎？）

常用單字成語

front	[frʌnt]	前面的
front desk		（飯店）服務台
wake up		叫醒
see to it		保證做到
menu		菜單
place		地點
nearby	[ˈnɪrˈbaɪ]	附近
maid	[med]	清潔女工
clean		打掃
absolutely	[ˈæbsəˌlutlɪ]	絕對
again		再次
as well		也

MP3-19

C in the restaurant
用餐

真實會話（在餐廳中…）

侍者：Is everything okay with your meal?
（您的餐飲一切都好吧？）

顧客：Yes, everything is fine.
（是的，各項都還好。）

Could you please bring me some more bread?
（可以請你再給我們送一些麵包過來嗎？）

侍者：Yes, sir. Would you like butter?
（可以，先生。您要奶油嗎？）

顧客：No. I still have some left.
（不用。我還有一些呢。）

侍者：I will bring that right away.
（我馬上就把麵包送過來。）

顧客：Thank you.
（謝謝你。）

增強美語實力

在餐廳服務的人，一定要會説 Is everything okay? 或 Is

everything all right?。這兩句美語是服務業的真言，每回走過顧客的身邊，就這樣問一句，保證小費多拿好幾成。

I still have some left.（我還剩一些。）的句型跟我們説話的習慣比較不同。要跟著錄音帶的老師示範多唸幾遍，熟了就自然會用。比較這兩種語言，我們習慣把「一些」這個詞放在句尾，而美語是把 left（剩下）留到最後才説，兩者有字序上的差異。但真正的困難是我們的語言沒有所謂「過去分詞」的詞類，所以很不習慣，也就很容易犯錯。歐美人説話的時候，習慣把形容東西屬性的形容詞如：顏色、大小等的字，加在名詞前面，如 red paper（紅紙）、big car（大車），跟我們的習慣相同，這方面沒有問題。可是，遇到形容一件事物「被」另一個事物的行為所影響，他們就喜歡用「過去分詞」來形容。例如：I still have some. 是「我還有一些。」，當要進一步形容這是「剩下的」一些時，他們就習慣用 leave（留）的過去分詞 left，表示還有一些「被我留著」。文法學家把這個語言現象解釋為 left 是「受詞補語」，補充説明受詞 some。筆者解釋文法，是希望有文法底子的讀者，可以融會貫通，同時藉以打破「英語會話沒有文法」的神話。可是，對自然學習語言的人，記太多文法名詞，是無助於語言的流利的。你還是跟著錄音帶老師的示範，多唸多用，自然就會了。

會話句型進階

Could you please bring me some more bread?
（可以請你幫我再送一些麵包過來嗎？）

» Can I get another glass of water?
（我可以再要一杯水嗎？）

» Could you please bring me another knife? This one is dirty.

（可以請你幫我送另外一隻餐刀來嗎？這一隻是髒的。）

» Could you get me another glass of wine?
（可以請你幫我再拿一杯酒嗎？）

加強小會話

顧客：Could you please bring me some more bread?
（可以請你幫我再送一些麵包過來嗎？）

侍者：There is a charge of $1.00.
（那要一美元的收費。）

Would you still like some?
（您還要嗎？）

常用單字成語

meal	[mil]	餐食
fine		好
bread	[brɛd]	麵包
butter	[ˈbʌtɚ]	奶油
right away		馬上；立刻
another	[əˈnʌðɚ]	另一個
knife	[naɪf]	刀
dirty	[ˈdɝtɪ]	髒的
wine		葡萄酒
charge	[tʃɑrdʒ]	費用
still		仍然

d in an office
上班

真實會話（同事找 Sally 要東西…）

A Hello, Sally.
（莎莉，妳好。）

B Hi, mike. How are you doing?
（嗨，麥克，你好嗎？）

A Pretty good.
（很好。）

Can I get that summary report from you?
（妳可以把綜合報告給我嗎？）

B Which one?
（哪個綜合報告？）

A The Ecuador summary.
（那一份「厄瓜多專案」的綜合報告。）

B Oh, sure.
（哦，沒有問題。）

I am working on two others as well.
（我另外還有兩個綜合報告在做呢。）

增強美語實力

向對方問好，習慣說 How are you? 的人，要特別注意本課。在國外，特別是在美國，How are you? 是有一段時間沒見面的親朋見面時說的。如果分別時間很久，又沒音訊，則再見面時會說 How have you been?，而對普通經常見面的人，不要說 How are you?，要說 How are you doing?、How is it going?、或 What's up?。下回看電影、電視，注意聽聽是不是這樣。

美語的 which 含有「哪一個？」的意思，暗示有幾樣選擇可以讓對方選一項。Which one? 則講得更明顯，指「你要哪一個？」。

I am working on two others as well. 的 as well 也是很多學了很多年美語的人不會用的。它的意思是「也」，放在句尾，大致上可以跟 too 互換。我們一般想到「也」就想到 too，所以不太會用 as well。too 大部份用在有人說一件事物，而你剛好「也」有這麼一件事物，這牽涉到兩個人。要是你說你在做一件事的同時，「也」在做另外的事，用 as well 比較好，它講的是同一個人做不同的事。

會話句型進階

Can I get that summary report from you?
（可以請你把那份綜合報告給我嗎？）

» Can I get you to type this up for me?
（可以請你幫我將這個打字嗎？）

» Can I get you to walk this down to the post box?
（可否請你拿這份東西走到郵筒去投寄呢？）

» Can I take a look at your work?
（我可以看看你的工作嗎？）

加強小會話

A Can I get that summary report from you?
（可以請你把綜合報告給我嗎？）

B No, it is not finished yet.
（不行，還沒有做完呢。）

常用單字成語

hello	[hə'lo]	（打招呼）喂
hi	[haɪ]	（熟人間打招呼）喂
work on		做
type		打字
type~up		（口語）把～打字
walk		步行
post box		郵筒
take a look		看一看
yet	[jɛt]	還；仍

MP3-21

e at a party
問路

真實會話（在宴會中，找洗手間…）

A Are you having a good time?
（你玩得愉快嗎？）

B I am, but I think my wife is a little uncomfortable.
（很愉快，不過我想我太太有些不自然。）

A It is always tough to meet people for the first time.
（第一次跟不熟的人相處，總是比較困難。）

B I know.
（我曉得。）

Could you please show me to the rest room?
（可否請你告訴我廁所在哪裡？）

A Sure. It is right across from us.
（當然。廁所就在我們對面那一邊。）

The second door to the left.
（向左轉第二道門就是。）

B Thanks. If you see my wife, feel free to show her around.
（謝謝你。要是你看見我太太的話，儘管帶她四處逛逛。）

增強美語實力

have a good time 是「玩得很開心」。這四個字要一起記，不過在實用上，have 的形式有變化：having a good time 表示「一直」玩得很快樂，而 had a good time 表示玩過了。使用這個說法時要看時間、場合，才不會用錯。例如：We had a good time tonight.（我們今晚玩得很開心。），這是玩過事後說的；We are having a good time tonight.（我們今晚玩得很開心。），這是還在玩的時候說的。

美語表示「同意」，可以說 I know.。雖然 know 是「知道」，但此地的用法，不在乎「知道什麼」，僅僅表示「我知道有這回事」、「我同意你的看法」而已。

學美語，盡量多用 feel free to 的句型。它是請對方不用客氣，儘管去做某件事。你想，在文明社會中用到這個句型的機會還會少嗎？Feel free to ask me.（儘管問我，沒關係。）、Feel free to call me.（儘管打電話給我。），對方聽到你說得這麼誠懇，心頭會覺得一陣熱的。

會話句型進階

Could you please show me to the rest room?
（可以請你告訴我廁所在哪裡嗎？）

» Could you please tell me where to pick up my coat?
（可以請你告訴我，我的外套放在哪裡？）

» Could you please get me another drink while you are over there?
（你到那邊的時候，是不是能幫我再拿一杯飲料？）

» Could you tell me where to throw away my

napkin?
（可否請你告訴我餐巾要丟在哪裡？）

加強小會話

A Could you please show me to the rest room?
（可否請你告訴我廁所在哪裡？）

B I can't. I don't even know myself.
（我不能告訴你。我自己都不知道在哪裡。）

Let's find Jack and ask him.
（我們還是找找傑克問他吧。）

常用單字成語

have a good time		玩得愉快
uncomfortable	[ən'kʌmfɚtəbl̩]	不自在
meet	[mit]	見面
people	['pipl̩]	人們
across		對面
second	['sɛkənd]	第二
to the left		在左邊
feel free		別客氣地（做某件事）
pick up		（口語）拿
coat	[kot]	外套
drink		飲料
napkin	['næpkɪn]	餐巾

5

asking for information

蒐集資訊美語

MP3-22

a about a product
購物

真實會話（購物時，查詢產品資料…）

顧客：I have never seen anything like this before.
（我從沒看過像這樣的東西。）

This is a great vacuum.
（這是個很好的吸塵器。）

推銷員：It is the newest design.
（它是最新的設計。）

顧客：Can I get some warranty information for this vacuum?
（可以給我這個吸塵器的保固資料嗎？）

推銷員：I will see what I can find.
（我來找一下看看有什麼資料。）

顧客：Do you know off the top of your head?
（你憑記憶所知，有沒有這方面的資料呢？）

推銷員：I am sorry. I don't.
（對不起。我不知道。）

We have only had those in for two days.
（這種吸塵器我們才剛進貨兩天。）

增強美語實力

購物是日常活動重要的一部份，所以有關購物的美語也要多學。

I have never seen anything like this. 的說法，不只在購物時用得上，在其他場合也可以用。have never seen 是「從未見過」，anything 可以指「東西」，也可以指「事情」，所以在購物的場合，它是「我從來沒有看過像這樣的東西」，而在一般日常生活，他就意味著「我從沒見過像這樣的事」。

產品的「保固」，也有人稱為「保證」，總之，是保證在一定期間內的產品耐用度，美語稱之為 warranty。另外一個很類似的字是guaranty，意思雖然也是「保證」，但它是一種個人「人格的保證」、「拍胸脯的保證」，與產品的「品質保證」不同。筆者見到很多我國的產品外銷到國外，英文產品保證書上寫著 guaranty，這是用錯字。

如果你懷疑用中學英文是否真的可以講流利的美語，你就來看 off the top of my head 這個詞。這些字，在初中二年級以前都學過了，off 是「出來」、「離開」的意思，top 是「上面」，head 是「頭」，組合起來就是「從我的頭出來」，也就是說話中常會用到的「憑我腦海裡的記憶」的意思，我們一般回應別人的詢問，如果不是很肯定，或是告訴對方我們的回答未經查證，就在句首或句尾帶上 off the top of my head.，這樣就可以了。

會話句型進階

Can I get some warranty information for this vacuum?
（可以給我一些這個吸塵器的保固資料嗎？）

» Can I get a brochure for this brand of paint?
（可以給我一份這種品牌油漆的說明書嗎？）

» Can I get a catalogue of other products?
（我可以要其它產品的型錄嗎？）

» Can I get someone to help me carry this out?
（我可以找個人幫我把這個東西帶出去嗎？）

加強小會話

顧客：Can I get some warranty information for this vacuum?
（可以給我一些關於這個吸塵器的保固資料嗎？）

推銷員：We are out of brochures, but there is some information in the owner's handbook.
（我們的說明書都用完了，不過在「使用手冊」裡，有一些這方面的資料。）

常用單字成語

vacuum	[ˈvækjʊəm]	吸塵器
design	[dɪˈzaɪn]	設計
warranty information		產品保固相關資料
off the top of your head		憑你記憶猜想
sorry	[ˈsɔrɪ]	對不起
brochure	[broˈʃjʊr]	說明書
brand		品牌
catalogue	[ˈkætḷˌɔg]	產品型錄
product	[ˈprɑdəkt]	產品
owner's handbook		使用手冊

b to rent a car
租車

真實會話（查詢費率⋯）

服務員：Welcome to Avis. How can I help you?
（歡迎光臨艾文絲租車公司。可以為您服務嗎？）

顧客：I need to get information about your daily rental rates.
（我需要一些關於你們每天租車費率的資料。）

服務員：We have a chart over there on the wall.
（在那邊的牆上我們掛有一份費率圖表。）

顧客：Do you have any brochures that I can take with me to the hotel?
（你們有沒有什麼說明書我可以帶回旅館的？）

服務員：Let me look in the back office.
（讓我到後面辦公室去看一看。）

顧客：Thank you.
（謝謝你。）

增強美語實力

How can I help you? 的 can 可以改說 may。How may I help you? 與 How can I help you? 意思和用法一模一樣，都是商業或公務上，接待來客的第一句話。舊式的說法是 Can I help you?（能為您效勞嗎？），現在是以服務掛帥，多用了一個 how，意思是「我已經決定為你效勞，請你告訴我效勞之處吧！」，服務的熱誠盡在這個 how 上展現。

rate 是「有關測量的單位」，在速度上指「速率」，在費用上，就是「費率」。rental rates 是「有關出租的費率」，適用於任何出租的行業，在租車公司，它指租車費率，在公寓，就是「每月或每年」的房租。

談費率，一定會用到 plan 這個字。你可能學過 plan 當成「計畫」的意思，例如 What's your plan?（你有什麼打算？），但在商業上談費率時，對方可能說明他們有不同的 plan，指的是不同「計算方法」，注意「加強小會話」中的例子。

會話句型進階

I need to get information about your daily rental rates.
（我需要一些關於你們每天租車費率的資料。）

» I need to get some rental information.
（我需要一些租車資料。）

» I need to get a listing of the cars you offer for rental.
（我需要一份你們供人租車的車型種類名單。）

» I need to get information about corporate account rentals.
（我需要關於公司戶頭租車的資料。）

加強小會話

顧客：I need to get information about your daily rental rates.
（我需要一份你們每天租車費率的資料。）

服務員：We have a variety of plans.
（我們有好幾種不同的租車方式。）

Do you know how long you need the car?
（你知道你要租多久嗎？）

常用單字成語

welcome	[ˈwɛlkəm]	歡迎
daily	[ˈdelɪ]	每日的
rental rates		租車費率
information		資訊
chart	[tʃɑrt]	圖表
back office		顧客不能進入的辦公室
listing	[ˈlɪstɪŋ]	名單
corporate account		公司客戶
variety	[vəˈraɪətɪ]	多樣的

MP3-24

C to rent an apartment.
租公寓

真實會話（詢問房屋格局…）

管理員：Good afternoon!
（午安！）

顧客：Hi. Is this the leasing office?
（嗨。這裡是出租辦公室嗎？）

管理員：Yes, it is. How can I help you?
（是的。有什麼為您服務之處嗎？）

顧客：Do you have any floor plan brochures?
（您有房間格局的説明書嗎？）

管理員：Yes, we have several.
（有，我們有一些。）

What size apartment are you looking for?
（您在找的是什麼樣大小的公寓呢？）

顧客：A two bedroom.
（兩房的公寓。）

增強美語實力

租房子屬於長期租約，所以美國話說 lease，與一般所謂的 rent（租）有些差別。不過，如果不是強調長期的租住，說 rent a house 也可以。

不論是 lease 或 rent 房子，房租還是稱為 rent。

美語稱房屋的格局為 floor plan，很容易記的。floor 是地板，或是樓房的樓層，plan 是當初建築的計畫，所以 floor plan 就是指格局而言。

會話句型進階

Do you have any floor plan brochures?
（你們有沒有房屋格局的說明書呢？）

» Do you have any information about the crime rate here?
（關於這裡的犯罪率你們有沒有什麼資料？）

» Do you have a listing of available apartments?
（你們有一份空公寓的列表嗎？）

» Do you have any short term rental information?
（你們有沒有什麼關於短期出租的資訊？）

加強小會話

顧客：Do you have any floor plan brochures?
（你們有沒有房屋格局的說明書？）

管理員：I am sorry. We are all out.
（對不起。我們全部都發完了。）

I can show you the model apartments if you like.
（如果你願意的話，我們可以讓你看樣品公寓。）

常用單字成語

leasing	['lisɪŋ]	租賃
leasing office		（公寓）管理員辦公室
floor plan		（房屋）格局
several	['sɛvrəl]	幾個
apartment	[ə'pɑrtmənt]	公寓
size		尺寸；大小
crime rate		犯罪率
available	[ə'veləbḷ]	可取得的
short term		短期
model	['mɑdḷ]	樣品

d flight information

訂機位

真實會話（打電話給航空公司…）

服務員：Eva Air, how may I direct your call?
（長榮航空公司，請問您找哪個部門？）

旅客：I want to confirm a flight schedule.
（我要確認班機行程。）

服務員：I can take care of that for you.
（那我可以幫您服務。）

旅客：Could you confirm flight 546 from Taipei to Singapore on January 23?
（可以請你確認一下一月二十三日從台北飛往新加坡的五四六號班機嗎？）

服務員：One moment....I show that flight leaving Taipei at 2:45 P.M.
（請稍待……我這裡顯示該班班機是下午兩點四十五分從台北起飛。）

旅客：Good. Thank you.
（那好。謝謝你。）

增強美語實力

所有的上班族都要特別注意 How may I direct your call? 的說法。這是接到公司外的人打電話進來時，應該馬上就問的一句話。direct 在這裡是轉接的意思。direct your call 指的是幫對方轉接電話，問對方 how（如何），就是要對方告訴你，他要找的是什麼人，或什麼部門。

叫人家等一等，可以說 one moment，也可以說 one second。moment 是短暫的一剎，second 是時間單位的「秒」，兩者都是講「一會兒」的意思。

在電話中，叫人家等一下，還有一種說法：hold on。上面提到的「稍待一會兒」one moment 和 one second 的說法，是普通場合都可以說的話，而在電話美語裡，可以叫對方「電話不要掛斷」，說法就是 hold on.。

會話句型進階

I want to confirm a flight schedule.
（我要確認班機的行程。）

» I want to check an arrival time for flight 567 at Beijing airport, today.
（我想要查一下今天五六七號班機抵達北京機場的時間。）

» I want to check seating availability on the next flight from Taipei to L.A.
（我要查一下，下一班班機從台北飛往洛杉磯還有沒有座位。）

» I want to see if I can reserve a seat on the next flight from Hong Kong to Sidney, Australia.
（我想要看看是否能在下一班從香港飛往澳州雪梨的班機上預訂一個座位。）

加強小會話

旅客：I want to confirm a flight schedule.
（我要確認班機行程。）

服務員： Hold one moment while I transfer your call.
（請不要掛斷電話稍待片刻，我幫你轉接。）

常用單字成語

direct	[də'rɛkt]	（電話）轉接
confirm	[kən'fɝm]	確認
flight schedule		班機時間表
Singapore		（國家）新加坡
January	['dʒænjʊ,ɛrɪ]	一月
moment		短暫的時間
arrival		抵達
availability	[ə,velə'bɪlətɪ]	可以取得
seating availability		有沒有機位
reserve	[rɪ'zɝv]	預訂
transfer	['trænsfɚ]	轉機
Australia		（國家）澳大利亞

MP3-26

e about accommodations
住飯店

真實會話（向飯店洽詢住宿資料…）

服務員：Sheraton Hotel, how may I help you?
（喜來登飯店，可以為你服務嗎？）

旅客：I need some information about your business suites.
（我要一些關於你們商務套房的資料。）

服務員：What would you like to know?
（你想要知道什麼呢？）

旅客：Do you have a direct phone line for laptop computers?
（你們的電話有沒有直接外線，可以給膝上型電腦使用？）

服務員：No, we do not.
（不，我們沒有。）

We have separate lines, but you have to dial 9 to get out.
（我們裝有分開的線路，不過你必須要先撥九才能打出去。）

旅客：I guess that doesn't matter.
（我想那不要緊吧。）

I have the same set-up at work.
（我在家裡的電話線也是這樣裝的。）

增強美語實力

在本課中學了一個很好用的句型：I need some information about...（我想跟你們要一些關於……的資料）。向任何機關或個人洽詢資料，都可以用這個句型。about 後面所接的名詞就是你所要的資料。

當然，我們一直強調語言是活的，說話的時候有各種不同的說法會讓對方感到與你談話很活潑，所以在「會話句型進階」裡，你可以針對洽詢資料多學幾句好用的美語說法。

會話句型進階

I need some information about your business suites.
（我需要一些關於你們商務套房的資料。）

» I need to find out what you have available next Tuesday.
（我想知道下星期二你們有什麼樣的空房。）

» I need to know where you are located.
（我要知道你們位於哪裡。）

» I need to get information about your shuttle services.
（我要知道你們車輛接送的資料。）

加強小會話

旅客：I need some information about your business suites.
（我要一些關於你們商務套房的資料。）

服務員：I'm sorry, we do not have business suites.
（對不起，我們沒有商務套房。）

Would you like to hear about our rooms?
（你想聽聽我們的客房種類嗎？）

常用單字成語

suite	[swit]	套房
business suites		商務套房
direct		直接的
separate	[ˈsɛpəret]	分開的
dial	[ˈdaɪəl]	（電話）撥號
matter	[ˈmætɚ]	有事
same		同樣的
set-up		裝置
find out		發覺
located	[ˈloketɪd]	位於
shuttle service		來回載客服務

6

Asking for location

旅遊問路美語

MP3-27

a to hotel
找旅館

真實會話（出國時，在機場問住宿旅館所在…）

旅客：Excuse me.
（對不起。）

服務員：How can I help you?
（可以為你服務嗎？）

旅客：Could you tell me where the Sheraton Hotel is?
（你可以告訴我喜來登飯店在哪裡嗎？）

服務員：There are two -- one downtown, and one here by the airport.
（喜來登飯店有兩家－－一家在市中心，另外一家就在機場這附近。）

旅客：I am staying at the one downtown.
（我要住在市中心的那一家。）

服務員：We have a shuttle that can take you there at no charge.
（我們有接送的車輛可以免費帶你到那裡。）

增強美語實力

說美國話時，要注意一種說法，文法上稱為「用現在進行式表示計畫性的未來」，像I am staying at the one downtown. 的說法。在這裡，「我選擇了市中心的飯店住」，是我的計畫，也是還沒有發生的事，在英文，這屬於「未來」的範疇，很多人可能因為事屬未來而直覺用I will stay at the one downtown. 的說法。可是，will stay 僅能表示未來，不表示我已經定了計畫，這兩者是有不同的。例如，I will go to New York. 的意思是「我要去紐約」，但不見得是已經計畫好前往的時間，而I am going to New York next Friday. 則是指「我要到紐約」，而且連「下星期五」這個離開的時間都定好了。

at no charge 是「免費」的意思。這裡的 charge 是「收費」，而表示費率的介係詞總是用 at，所以不收費就說成 at no charge。

會話句型進階

Could you tell me where the Sheraton Hotel is?
（你可以告訴我喜來登飯店在哪裡嗎？）

» Could you give me directions to the Sheraton Hotel?
（你可以告訴我喜來登飯店怎麼走嗎？）

» Could you tell me where to go to get a shuttle to the Sheraton?
（你可以告訴我到哪裡搭來往運送的車輛到喜來登飯店嗎？）

» Could you help me find the Sheraton Hotel?
（你可以告訴我如何找到喜來登飯店嗎？）

加強小會話

旅客：Could you tell me where the Sheraton Hotel is?
（你可以告訴我喜來登飯店在哪裡嗎？）

服務員：I don't know, but the information booth is over there.
（我不知道在哪裡，不過詢問台就在那邊。）

常用單字成語

excuse	[ɪk'skjuz]	原諒
downtown		市中心
shuttle	['ʃʌtḷ]	（飯店、機場）來回載客車輛
no charge		免費
directions	[də'rɛkʃənz]	方向指示
booth	[buθ]	攤位
information booth		詢問台
over there		在那邊

MP3-28

b to the airport

前往機場

真實會話（在國外問路…）

A Are you from around here?
（你是住在附近的人嗎？）

B Yes, why do you ask?
（是的，你為何有此一問呢？）

A Can you tell me the best way to get to the airport?
（可否請你告訴我到飛機場的最好的走法？）

B Sure. Do you have something for me to write with?
（當然。你有沒有東西可以讓我用來寫呢？）

A Yes, let me get it from my car.
（有，我到車上去拿。）

B It is really easy to get there.
（到飛機場是很簡單的。）

增強美語實力

介係詞 around 指「四周」，所以不論是時間或是地點，凡是跟「鄰近」有關的意念都可用 around。例如 around 9 o'clock（九點左右），around the school（學校附近）。由此可知，「住在這附近的人」就是 someone from around here。

我們學過用 Can you...□ 的句型請人家幫忙，下面的「會話句型進階」有幾個類似的說法，但請勿忽略，美語的 can you...? 不僅僅能用來請人幫忙，別忘了它的原意是問「可不可以……？」，例如「會話句型進階」的第二句，就是在問沿著一條路「能不能」抵達機場。

會話句型進階

Can you tell me the best way to get to the airport?
（可否請你告訴我到飛機場的最好走法？）

» Can you give me directions to the airport?
（您是否可以告訴我飛機場在哪裡？）

» Can you get to the airport on this road?
（從這一條路可以到得了飛機場嗎？）

» Can you draw me a map to the airport?
（你可以幫我畫一張到飛機場的地圖嗎？）

加強小會話

A Can you tell me the best way to get to the airport?
（可否請你告訴我到飛機場的最好走法？）

B No, but I know someone who can.
（不行，不過我知道有人可以。）

常用單字成語

around here		在這附近
way		方法
the best way		最好的方法
airport	[ˈɛrˌport]	機場
easy	[ˈizɪ]	容易
road	[rod]	路
draw	[drɔ]	畫
map		地圖
draw (someone) a map		幫（某人）畫地圖

C to the shopping areas
購物

真實會話（當有人問路時⋯）

A You seem to have settled in.
（你好像已經安頓妥當。）

Do you have any questions?
（你有什麼問題嗎？）

B Yes. Where is the nearest shopping mall?
（有。最靠近的購物中心在哪裡呢？）

A Do you need anything specific?
（你有沒有特別要買什麼東西？）

B I will need more clothes while I am here.
（在這裡我必須要增添一些衣物。）

A The best place to go is the mall downtown.
（那最好的去處是市中心的購物中心。）

B If you could give me directions, I would appreciate it.
（如果你可以告訴我怎麼走，我會非常感激。）

增強美語實力

亞洲的移民多，經濟商務也發達，派駐外國的上班族，外國公司來駐的英美人士也多，settle in 這個詞用上的自然也多。settle 的原意指「解決」而言，但 settle in 卻是指新到一個地方的人「安頓妥當」。所以你若是認識剛到本地的人，不妨用 Have you settled in?（都安頓好了嗎？）、或 You seem to have settled in.（你似乎都安頓妥當了。）作為說話的開場白。

請別人指引你方向，可以套用學過的 Can you 的句型，直接說 Can you give me directions?（你可以指引我方向嗎？），本課我們要學一個很能表現說話者素養的活用句型。首先，用 if 來起頭，把 can 改成 could，變成 If you could give me directions（假如你可以指引我方向的話），然後加上一句 I would appreciate it（我會很感激）。這個說法非常客氣，是受過教育的人、有涵養的人用的句型。例如，請人家別抽煙，可以說 If you could stopped smoking here, I would appreciate it. 這個說法也可以先說 I would appreciate it 再說 if 的部份。

會話句型進階

If you could give me directions, I would appreciate it.
（如果你可以告訴我如何走的話，我會非常感激。）

» I would appreciate it if you could show me the way downtown.
（如果你可以告訴我到市中心的走法，我會非常感激。）

» If you could tell me where to find a place to shop, I would appreciate it.
（如果你可以告訴我哪裡可以找到購物的地方，我會很感激。)

» If you could direct me to the mall, I would appreciate it.
(如果你可以指引我到購物中心,我會很感激。)

加強小會話

A If you could give me directions, I would appreciate it.
(如果你可以告訴我如何走的話,我會很感激。)

B I am not the best with directions.
(指引方向我不是最好的人選。)

Let me draw you a map.
(讓我幫你畫份地圖吧。)

常用單字成語

settle	[ˈsɛtl̩]	解決
settle in		安頓妥當
question	[ˈkwɛstʃən]	問題
shopping mall		大型購物中心
specific	[spɪˈsɪfɪk]	特定的
clothes	[kloðz]	衣物
appreciate	[əˈpriʃɪˌet]	感激
show (someone) the way		幫(某人)指路

MP3-30

d to the tourist spots

帶人觀光

真實會話（對外國朋友盡地主之誼…）

A How do you like Taipei so far?
（截至目前為止，你還喜歡台北嗎？）

B Pretty good.
（非常好。）

I still don't know what to do after work, though.
（不過下了班我還是不知道要幹什麼。）

A There is a lot of stuff to do.
（有好多事可以做的。）

B Can you tell me where all the good spots are?
（你可以告訴我所有的好地方都在哪裡嗎？）

A Sure. In fact, I can take you around to most of them this weekend.
（當然了。事實上，我這個週末可以帶你到大部份的好地方去看。）

B That sounds great.
（那好極了。）

增強美語實力

I can do even better是純美國話，指的是「我還可以做得更徹底」，它可以用在任何會話場合，例如有人跟你借錢，你除了說Yes「沒問題」之外，你還可以說I can do even better -- you don't need to pay me back.（我還可以做得讓你更高興，你可以不需要還我錢。」

會話句型進階

Can you tell me where all the good spots are?
（你可以告訴我所有的好地方都在哪裡嗎？）

» Can you tell me where I should go for fun?
（你可以告訴我哪裡可以去玩嗎？）

» Can you tell me what most visitors go to see?
（你可以告訴我大部份遊客都到哪裡去觀光嗎？）

» Can you tell me what sights are best to see.
（你可以告訴我最好的觀光點是在哪裡嗎？）

加強小會話

A Can you tell me where all the good spots are?
（你可以告訴我所有的好地點都在哪裡嗎？）

B I can do even better--I'll take you to them.
（我不僅可以告訴你，我還可以帶你去。）

常用單字成語

so far		到目前
after work		下班後
a lot of stuff		很多事情
spot	[spɑt]	（口語）地點
in fact		事實上
for fun		好玩
visitor	[ˈvɪzɪtɚ]	訪客
sight	[saɪt]	風景區
even		甚至

e of medical facilities

醫療設施在哪裡？

真實會話（關照外國朋友生活…）

A Have you been doing well?
（你一切都還好吧？）

B Yes, I have.
（是的，都好。）

A Do you have a good idea of where everything is at in town?
（你對本市的各地都已經有個良好的概念了嗎？）

B Almost.
（幾乎都有了。）

Where is the nearest emergency medical center?
（最靠近的緊急醫療中心在哪裡呢？）

A There is a hospital on Main Street.
（緬因街上有一間醫院。）

There is also an emergency clinic two blocks from the office.
（從我們辦公室出去過兩條街也有一個緊急診所。）

B It is good to know where a hospital is at in case I get sick.
（萬一我生病的話，知道醫院在哪裡是很好的。）

增強美語實力

clinic是「診所」，是一個或幾個醫師一起開設的看病的地方，多半僅有基本醫療設備，也沒有供住院的床位，而hospital才是真正的醫院，各科皆備，設備齊全，也可住院。兩者不同，在說美語的時候，不要凡是上醫院都用hospital，英美人士會以為你害了大病或急證。

clinic在口語上說成doctor's office。所以一般去看醫生，都說go see a doctor，或是go to the doctor's office。

會話句型進階

Where is the nearest emergency medical center?
（最靠近的緊急醫療中心在哪裡？）

» Where should I go if I need medical help?
（我如果需要醫療協助的話，應該到哪裡去呢？）

» Where is the nearest hospital?
（最靠近的醫院在哪裡呢？）

» Where is a good doctor's office?
（好的醫生診所在哪裡呢？）

加強小會話

A Where is the nearest emergency medical center?
（最靠近的緊急醫療中心在哪裡呢？）

B I would feel better if I showed you.
（我親自帶你去會覺得踏實一點。）

That way you know for sure.
（那樣的話，我可以確定你確實知道在哪裡。）

常用單字成語

idea	[aɪ′diə]	概念
almost	[′ɔlmost]	幾乎
emergency	[ɪ′mɝdʒənsɪ]	緊急
medical center		醫療中心
hospital	[′hɑspɪtl̩]	醫院
clinic	[′klɪnɪk]	診所
block	[blɑk]	（市區裡）街段
in case		萬一
get sick		生病
doctor's office		診所
for sure		確定

7

express concern

表示關切的美語

MP3-32

a asking what is the matter

表示關心

真實會話（朋友看來心情不好…）

A Hi, John, how are you doing?
（嗨，約翰，你好嗎？）

B Okay, I guess.
（我想還好吧。）

A You sound down.
（你聽起來情緒不佳。）

What's the matter?
（怎麼啦？）

B Oh, my son Robert is doing poorly in school.
（哦，我兒子羅伯在學校表現很差。）

A Is his behavior bad?
（他的行為不好嗎？）

B No, he is a good kid.
（不，他是個好孩子。）

He is having trouble in reading, and it is slowing him down.
（他閱讀有問題，所以功課就比較趕不上。）

會話句型進階

What's the matter?

（怎麼了？）

» What is bothering you?
（有什麼事在困擾著你呢？）

» What's on your mind?
（你心裡在想什麼呢？）

» What is worrying you?
（你在擔心什麼呢？）

加強小會話

A What's the matter?
（怎麼了？）

B I appreciate your concern, but I don't want to talk about it right now.
（我很感謝你的關心，不過我現在不想談這件事。）

常用單字成語

down		（口語）沮喪
matter		事務
poorly	[ˈpʊrlɪ]	很糟
in school		在學校
behavior	[bɪˈhevjɚ]	行為
have trouble in~		對（某事）有困難
bother	[ˈbɑðɚ]	困擾
on (someone's) mind		（某人的）心思
worry	[ˈwɝɪ]	擔憂
concern	[kənˈsɝn]	關心

MP3-33

b giving tentative advice
提建議

真實會話（朋友心裡有掛慮…）

A I am worried about my son's reading problem.
（我為我兒子的閱讀問題感到擔憂。）

B Do you mind if I make a suggestion?
（如果我給你一項建議你會介意嗎？）

A Not at all.
（我不會介意的。）

B You might have him tested for word blindness.
（你可能要讓他檢查一下是否犯了字盲。）

A We have thought about that.
（我們也曾經想過。）

B I know it can be tough to admit that your child has a problem.
（我知道要承認小孩有困難是很為難的事。）

It was for us.
（我們自己就是這樣。）

會話句型進階

Do you mind if I make a suggestion?
（如果我給你一項建議的話你會不會介意？）

» Do you mind if I give you some advice?
（如果我給你一些忠言你會不會介意？）

» Can I give you my input?
（我可以給你我的想法嗎？）

» You might consider doing this way.
（你可能要考慮這樣做。）

加強小會話

A Do you mind if I make a suggestion?
（如果我給你做一項建議你會介意嗎？）

B Don't take it personal, but we are already flooded with ideas from other people.
（我這句話不是衝著你個人而來，不過我們已經從別人那裡得到很多點子了。）

常用單字成語

suggestion	[sə'dʒɛstʃən]	建議
blindness	['blaɪndnɪs]	盲
word blindness		字盲症
thought		想（think 的過去式）
admit		承認
advice	[əd'vaɪs]	忠告
input		見解
consider	[kən'sɪdɚ]	考慮
take (something) personal		認為（某事）是針對個人而來
flood		氾濫

MP3-34

C giving advice not to do something

提出警告

真實會話（有人要出外旅遊…）

A I am thinking of going skiing for the Christmas holiday.
（我打算耶誕節假期要去滑雪。）

B Are you going to take the whole family?
（你要帶著全家去嗎？）

A Of course!
（那當然！）

B I wouldn't do that if I were you.
（要是我是你的話，我不會這樣做的。）

A Why not?
（為何不呢？）

B If you haven't made reservations before now, all of the lift tickets will be sold.
（如果到現在你還沒有預訂的話，所有上山的票都已經賣完了。）

會話句型進階

I wouldn't do that if I were you.
（我若是你的話，我就不會這樣做。）

» I would think twice before doing that.
（做那件事以前我是會再考慮的。）

» I don't think that would be a good thing to do.
（我不認為那樣做是好的。）

» I would really advise against that.
（我真的要警告你不要那樣做。）

加強小會話

A I wouldn't do that if I were you.
（我若是你的話，我就不會那樣做。）

B Well, you are not me.
（是嘛，只可惜你不是我。）

常用單字成語

Christmas	[ˈkrɪsməs]	耶誕節
holiday	[ˈhɑləde]	假日
whole		全部
reservation	[ˌrɛzɚˈveʃən]	預訂
lift		（滑雪）上山的吊椅
ticket	[ˈtɪkɪt]	票
think twice		三思而後行
advise	[ədˈvaɪz]	警告

MP3-35

d general concern

關心的話

真實會話（同事很累的樣子…）

A Are you okay, Mike? You look tired.
（麥克，你還好嗎？你看起來很累。）

B I was up all night with my mother in the hospital.
（我整個晚上沒有睡覺，在醫院陪我母親。）

A How is she doing?
（她的情況如何？）

B They don't think she will live.
（他們不認為她可以活下來。）

A I am sorry to hear that.
（很遺憾聽到這個消息。）

Why don't you take the day off?
（你今天怎麼不請假呢？）

B I thought I would be able to take my mind off of it by working.
（我認為上班可以讓我的心思從那件事情上移開。）

會話句型進階

Are you okay, Mike?
（麥克，你還好嗎？）

» Is everything all right?
（每樣事情都還好吧？）

» Are you feeling well?
（你覺得不舒服嗎？）

» Have you been doing okay?
（你一向都好嗎？）

加強小會話

A Are you okay, Mike?
（麥克，你還好吧？）

B Yes, much better.
（是的，好多了。）

Thank you for asking.
（謝謝你的關心。）

常用單字成語

tired	[taɪrd]	疲倦
(be) up all night		（口語）一夜未睡
sorry	[ˈsɔrɪ]	遺憾
all right		很好
feel		感覺
better	[ˈbɛtɚ]	比較好
much better		好多了

MP3-36

e helping concern

自願幫忙

真實會話（對方可能有事需要幫忙…）

A I don't know how much longer my mother will make it.
（我不知道我母親還可以撐多久。）

B Is there anything I can do?
（我可以幫你什麼忙嗎？）

A Not really, but I appreciate the offer.
（幫不上忙，不過我還是很感激你的提議。）

B I know that it is really hard on the kids at the hospital.
（我知道在醫院裡對小孩子來說是很困難的事。）

A It is. I might ask you to watch them if you don't mind.
（真的。如果你不介意的話，我可能會請你幫我看小孩。）

B I would be glad to help.
（我很樂意幫忙的。）

會話句型進階

Is there anything I can do?
（有什麼我可以盡力之處嗎？）

» Can I help in any way?
（我可以在任何方面幫忙嗎？）

» Is there anything you need?
（你需要什麼嗎？）

» Do you need me to cover any of your work?
（你需要我幫你代班嗎？）

加強小會話

A Is there anything I can do for you?
（有什麼我可以幫你效勞之處嗎？）

B Yes, please answer my phone while I am away.
（有，當我不在的時候，請幫我接電話。）

常用單字成語

longer	['lɔŋgɚ]	比較久
make it		（口語）撐得住；做成功
appreciate	[ə'priʃɪˌet]	感激
watch		看管
be glad to~		樂意做（某事）
help		幫助
cover	['kʌvɚ]	（口語）代班
answer	['ænsɚ]	回答

8

Ask what to do

要求指導的美語

MP3-37

a asking the procedure
詢問程序

真實會話（剛接新的職務時…）

A Are you about ready to start taking inventory?
（你準備好可以開始盤點存貨了嗎？）

B How should I go about cataloging the merchandise?
（我應該如何登錄這些商品呢？）

A You want to count the number of items on the shelf and in boxes.
（你必須數架上和盒裡的各項東西有幾個。）

B What then?
（然後呢？）

A Write in the number next to the item name, and cross it off your work list.
（在品名的旁邊寫下那個數字，然後從你的工作表上面把那一個項目劃掉。）

B Okay, thanks for your help.
（好，謝謝你的幫忙。）

會話句型進階

How should I go about cataloging the merchandise?
（我該如何登記這些商品呢？）

» How should I address the letter?
（這封信的抬頭我應該註明是誰呢？）

» How should I start writing the report?
（我應該如何下筆寫報告呢？）

» How should I begin the project?
（這個專案我應該如何開始呢？）

加強小會話

A How should I go about cataloging the merchandise?
（我應該如何登錄這些商品呢？）

B The instructions are on the back page.
（這在登記單背頁有說明。）

常用單字成語

inventory	[ˈɪnvəntorɪ]	存貨
take inventory		盤點存貨
catalog	[ˈkætlˌɔg]	登錄
merchandise	[ˈmɝtʃənˌdaɪz]	貨物
count		點算
cross it off		將某行字畫掉
work list		工作細目
address	[əˈdrɛs]	v.（信件）註明收件人
instructions	[ɪnˈstrʌkʃənz]	說明
back page		（紙頁的）背面

MP3-38

b asking what the requirements are
應徵工作

真實會話（找工作…）

求事者：I am getting ready to fill out my application.
（我準備好可以填申請表了。）

人事員：If you need any help, let me know.
（如果你需要協助，讓我知道。）

求事者：What are the requirements of the position?
（這個職位的要求條件是什麼？）

人事員：To be able to answer calls for Mr. Smith, and to type any letters he might need.
（要能幫史密斯先生接電話，而且在他有信需要打字時，幫他打字。）

求事者：Should I put down other experience, too?
（我也得要寫下我其他的工作經驗嗎？）

人事員：I am sure that any information will be helpful.
（我肯定認何資訊都是有幫助的。）

會話句型進階

What are the requirements of the position?
（本職位所要求的資格是什麼？）

» What is required to complete the course?
（要完成這門課有什麼需求？）

» What are the requirements for admission?
（要申請入學有什麼條件？）

» What will we need to do to be accepted?
（我們需要做什麼才能夠被接受呢？）

加強小會話

求事者：What are the requirements of the position?
（本職位所需要的條件是什麼？）

人事員：The job description is posted on the wall behind you.
（在你背後的牆上貼有職務説明。）

常用單字成語

fill out		（表格）填
application	[ˌæpləˈkeʃən]	申請表
requirement	[rɪˈkwaɪrmənt]	資格要求
position	[pəˈzɪʃən]	職位
put down		寫
experience	[ɪkˈspɪrɪəns]	經驗

helpful		有幫助的
complete	[kəm'plit]	完成
course		課目
admission	[əd'mɪʃən]	入學許可
accept		接受
job description		職務說明
posted		張貼出來

MP3-39

C asking whether something is permitted
請求許可

真實會話（抽煙之前，徵求許可…）

A How are you doing, John?
（約翰，你好嗎？）

B Good. Yourself?
（很好。你自己呢？）

A I am doing just fine.
（我還不錯。）

Is it okay for me to smoke?
（我抽煙可以嗎？）

B No, we cannot smoke in the building anymore.
（不行，我們不能夠再在大樓裡抽煙了。）

A I have been out of the office for so long!
（我離開公司太久了！）

It seems that everything has been changed.
（似乎樣樣事情都已經改變了。）

B It just takes a little time to get used to being

back in the states.
（回到美國，是需要一些時間才能適應的。）

會話句型進階

Is it okay for me to smoke?
（我抽煙可以嗎？）

» Is it all right to leave my car here?
（我把車子留在這裡可以嗎？）

» Is it okay to bring my kids to the company party?
（把我的小孩帶到公司的宴會可以嗎？）

» Is early voting allowed here?
（本地允許提前投票嗎？）

加強小會話

A Is it okay for me to smoke?
（我抽煙可以嗎？）

B Yes, we have a break room down the hall.
（可以的，這條走道過去一點，我們有一間休息室在那裡。）

常用單字成語

smoke		抽煙
building	[ˈbɪldɪŋ]	大樓
not ... anymore		不能再（做某事）
out of the office		（商業口語）出差

change	[tʃendʒ]	改變
get used to		習慣於
in the states		在美國
company party		公司辦的宴會
early voting		（選舉）提早投票
allowed	[ə'laʊd]	被允許的
break room		（員工的）休息室

MP3-40

d asking whether something is recommended

徵求意見

真實會話（看醫生之前，詢問意見…）

A I am thinking of going to doctor White for a check-up.
（我打算要到懷特醫生那裡去檢查一下。）

B I hear he is a good doctor.
（我聽說他是個好醫師。）

A Do you think I should get a flu shot while I am there?
（你認為我找他的時候，應該打個感冒預防針嗎？）

B I think it as a very good idea.
（我認為那是個很好的主意。）

A Do you get them yourself?
（你自己有沒有打預防針呢？）

B Every year!
（每年都打！）

會話句型進階

Do you think I should get a flu shot while I am there?
（你認為當我在那裡的時候，是否應該接受感冒預防針的注射？）

» Do you recommend that I call the boss before I go up there?
（在我上去找老闆之前，你看我是不是先打個電話給他比較好？）

» Do you think it is better to make reservations, or wait until I get there?
（你認為先訂座比較好，還是等我到了那裡再說？）

» Do you know if it is a good idea to go there for vacation?
（你知道到那裡去度假是不是好主意呢？）

加強小會話

A Do you think I should get a flu shot while I am there?
（你認為我在那裡時應該接受感冒預防注射嗎？）

B I don't know. I have never done it.
（我不知道。我自己從沒打過。）

常用單字成語

doctor	[ˈdɑktɚ]	醫生
check-up		檢查
flu shot		流行感冒預防針
while		當
recommend	[ˌrɛkəˈmɛnd]	推薦
boss		主管
wait until~		等到～才
vacation	[vəˈkeʃən]	假期

MP3-41

e asking whether something is liked

喜不喜歡

真實會話（出國旅遊之前，問別人經驗…）

A Have you ever been to Disney World?
（你有沒有到過狄斯耐世界？）

B Yes, I went there last summer.
（去過，我去年夏天去過。）

A Did you like it?
（你喜歡那個地方嗎？）

B I thought it was fantastic!
（我認為那個地方太好了！）

A Would you go there again?
（你會再去嗎？）

B If I could get the time off, I would go.
（如果我可以找到時間請假，我會去的。）

會話句型進階

Would you go there again?
（你會再去嗎？）

» Would it be a good idea to go?
（去那裡會是個好主意嗎？）

» Would I have a good time?
（我會玩得愉快嗎？）

» Would you go back?
（你還會再去嗎？）

加強小會話

A Would you go there again?
（你會再去那個地方嗎？）

B It was fun, but there are other places I want to see.
（那個地方是好玩，不過我還有其他的地方要看。）

常用單字成語

world	[wɝld]	世界
summer	[ˈsʌmɚ]	夏天
last summer		去年夏天
fantastic	[fænˈtæstɪk]	太美妙了
again		再度
get the time off		可以請假
fun		好玩

9

asking opinion

尋求意見的美語

a about medical care
就醫

真實會話（在國外，請人介紹醫生…）

A Are you familiar with doctors here?
（你對這裡的醫師熟嗎？）

B Yes, I know quite a few of them.
（是的，我是認識好幾個醫生。）

A Who do you recommend I take my kids to?
（你建議我應該帶我的小孩去看哪一個醫生呢？）

B I think Dr. Martin is a great pediatrician.
（我想馬丁醫生是很好的小兒科醫生。）

A You are the second person to tell me that.
（你是第二個人這樣告訴我的。）

B She is very good with children.
（她對小孩子非常親切的。）

會話句型進階

Who do you recommend I take my kids to?
（你建議我帶小孩去看哪一位醫生呢？）

» Who do you think is a good doctor?

（你認為哪一位是個好醫生呢？）

» Who is a good dentist?
（哪一位是好的牙科醫師呢？）

» Who is a good vet to take my dog to?
（我應該帶我的狗去看哪一位好的獸醫呢？）

加強小會話

A Who do you recommend I take my kids to?
（你建議我應該帶我小孩去看哪一位醫生呢？）

B I am not sure.
（我不太肯定。）

My wife really takes care of that.
（都是我太太在照顧那一方面的事的。）

常用單字成語

familiar	[fə'mɪljɚ]	熟悉
quite		非常
quite a few		數目不少
pediatrician	[,pidɪə'trɪʃən]	小兒科醫生
second		第二的
person		人
children	['tʃɪldrn̩]	兒童（child 的複數）
dentist		牙醫
vet		獸醫（veterinarian 的縮寫）

b politics
政治

真實會話（與時事有關的話題⋯）

A Have you kept up with the presidential race?
（你有沒有在密切注意總統選舉？）

B Yes. I keep up with all of the elections.
（有。我對所有的選舉都密切注意。）

A What is your opinion of the congressional candidate?
（你對這位國會議員候選人有什麼看法？）

B I think he is a good man, but he does not have enough experience.
（我認為他人是很好，但是他的經驗不夠。）

A Neither did the founding fathers.
（我們的開國元勳也沒什麼經驗。）

B Good point.
（那倒是不錯。）

會話句型進階

What is your opinion of the congressional candidate?
（你對這位國會議員候選人有什麼看法？）

» Do you agree with his views on education?
（你同意他對教育的觀點嗎？）

» Which candidate do you prefer?
（你比較喜歡哪一位候選人？）

» What's your view on his tax cut promise?
（你對他承諾要減稅一事有什麼看法？）

加強小會話

A What is your opinion of the congressional candidate?
（你對這位國會議員候選人有什麼看法？）

B It is hard to say.
（那很難說。）

I think it will be a close race, though.
（不過，我認為那會是一個很接近的選戰。）

常用單字成語

keep up with		密切注意
presidential	[ˌprɛzəˈdɛnʃəl]	總統的
race		競賽；選情
election	[ɪˈlɛkʃən]	選舉
congressional	[kənˈgrɛʃənəl]	國會的

candidate	[ˈkændə͵det]	候選人
neither		也不
founding fathers		開國元勳
education	[͵ɛdʒəˈkeʃən]	教育
prefer		較喜歡的
tax cut		減稅
close		相近的

MP3-44

C social

一般交往會話

真實會話（想上餐廳⋯）

A Have you eaten at the new Italian restaurant down the road?
（街上下去那一間新開的義大利餐館，你去吃過沒有？）

B Yes, my wife and I ate there last weekend.
（吃過了，我和我太太上個星期週末去吃過了。）

A Do you recommend it?
（你會推薦我們去嗎？）

B Yes, the food and service are great.
（是的，食物和服務都很好。）

It is a little expensive, though.
（不過，它們可是有點貴。）

A I guess it's probably not a good place to take the kids.
（我想那裡大概不是一個帶小孩子去的好地方吧。）

B No, I don't think they would like the kind of food they serve.
（不，我不認為小孩子會喜歡他們那裡所供應的食物。）

會話句型進階

Do you recommend it?

（你會推薦我們去嗎？）

» Which Italian restaurant do you recommend, the one downtown or next door?
（你推薦哪一家義大利餐館，是去市區的那一家還是隔壁這一家？）

» Where do you recommend we go for a quiet dinner?
（你建議我們到哪兒去吃一頓寧靜的晚餐？）

» Do you recommend the restaurant across the street?
（你建議我們到對街的那一家餐館嗎？）

加強小會話

A Do you recommend it?
（你建議我們去嗎？）

B No, we had bad service, and the price was too high.
（不，我們獲得的服務很不好，而且價格也太貴。）

常用單字成語

Italian	[ɪ'tæljən]	義大利的
restaurant	['rɛstərənt]	餐館
wife		妻
ate		吃（eat 的過去式）

food and service		（餐館的）菜色與服務
expensive	[ɪk'spɛnsɪv]	昂貴的
serve		服務的
next door		隔壁
quiet		安靜的
street		街道

d hair salon

美容

真實會話（請人推薦美容院…）

A Can you recommend a good hair salon?
（你可以推薦一家好的髮廊嗎？）

B Yes, you should try Studio 100.
（可以的，你應該試一下 100 工作室。）

A Is that where you get your hair cut?
（你就是在那個地方剪頭髮的嗎？）

B Yes, I have gone there for years.
（是的，好幾年以來我都是在那個地方剪的。）

A Who should I schedule an appointment with?
（我應該跟誰約時間呢？）

B Ask for Amy Lee.
（你要約李艾美。）

She does a great job.
（她的手藝非常好。）

會話句型進階

Can you recommend a good hair salon?
（你可以推薦一家好的髮廊嗎？）

» I need a haircut and manicure, do you have any recommendations?
（我需要剪頭髮和修指甲，你有沒有什麼好的可以推薦呢？）

» Can you recommend a good place to get my hair permed?
（你可以推薦一個好地方讓我燙頭髮嗎？）

» I need a new style. Where is a good salon?
（我需要做一個新髮型。哪一家是好髮廊呢？）

加強小會話

A Can you recommend a good hair salon?
（你可以建議一家好的髮廊嗎？）

B Not really. I have my wife cut my hair.
（沒辦法。我的頭髮都是我太太剪的。）

常用單字成語

salon	[sə′lɑn]	美容院
hair salon		髮型屋；髮廊
cut		剪
studio	[′stjʊdɪˏo]	工作室；攝影棚
schedule	[′skɛdʒʊl]	定時間
appointment	[ə′pɔɪntmənt]	約會
haircut		剪髮
recommendation	[ˏrɛkəmən′deʃən]	推薦
perm		燙髮
style		髮型

e mechanic
修車

真實會話 (汽車故障了…)

A I'm having trouble with my brakes again.
（我車子的剎車又有問題了。）

B Do you know what the problem is?
（你知道問題出在哪裡嗎？）

A Yes, but I can't find a good mechanic.
（我知道，可是我找不到一個好的修理技工。）

Where is a good place to go?
（哪裡是個可以修車的好地方呢？）

B You should go to Lee's Garage.
（你應該去試試李氏修車廠。）

A Have you had any work done by him?
（你有沒有在他那邊修過車？）

B Yeah, he is the only person I let touch my car.
（有啊，我只讓他一個人動我的車。）

會話句型進階

Where is a good place to go?

（哪裡是可以去修車的好地方？）

» Where is the best place to have my tires rotated at a reasonable price?
（哪裡是最好的地方，可以用合理的價格做輪胎平衡換位呢？）

» Where should I go for an oil change in less than twenty minutes?
（我該去哪裡，可以在二十分鐘之內換好機油呢？）

» Who do you think is the best mechanic for standard transmissions?
（你認為哪一位是修手排檔的最好技師呢？）

加強小會話

A Where is a good place to go?
（哪裡是可以修車的好地方呢？）

B Call Lee's Garage.
（打電話給李氏修車廠。）

They do good work.
（他們的工作做的很好。）

常用單字成語

brake		（車輛的）剎車系統
mechanic	[məˈkænɪk]	汽車修理工
garage	[gəˈrɑʒ]	修車場
let		讓

touch		觸摸
rotate	[ˈrotet]	（車胎）平衡換位
reasonable	[ˈriznəbl̩]	合理的
less than		少於
standard	[ˈstændɚd]	標準
transmission	[trænsˈmɪʃən]	（車輛）排檔
standard transmissions		手排檔

10

Talking about the past events

用過去式說美語

MP3-47

a remembering

談往事

真實會話 (過去的事…)

A Remember when it only cost two dollars to go to the movies?
(你還記得去看一場電影只花兩美元的時候嗎?)

B I sure do.
(我當然記得。)

A You could also get popcorn and a coke for a dollar.
(你還可以只花一美元就買得到爆玉米花和一杯可樂。)

B I remember.
(我還記得。)

All you needed was three dollars and a free afternoon.
(全部所需要的只是三塊錢和一個空閒的下午。)

A Now it cost ten dollars for a movie and refreshments.
(現在去看一場電影買一點點心就要花十美元了。)

B I know.
(我知道。)

It has gotten expensive.
（看電影越來越貴了。）

會話句型進階

Remember when it only cost two dollars to go to the movies?
（還記得去看一場電影只花兩美元的時候嗎？）

» Remember when we worked the late shift at the hospital?
（還記得我們在醫院裡做大夜班嗎？）

» Remember our senior year of high school?
（記得我們高三那一年嗎？）

» Remember when we won the gold medal two years in a row?
（記得我們連續兩年贏得金牌嗎？）

加強小會話

A Remember when it only cost two dollars to go to the movies?
（記得去看一場電影只花兩美元的時候嗎？）

B No, I have not lived here that long.
（不，我在這裡還沒有住那麼久呢。）

常用單字成語

remember	[rɪ'mɛmbɚ]	記得
go to the movies		看電影

popcorn	[ˈpɑpˌkɔrn]	爆玉米花
dollar		美元
free		空閒的
refreshments	[rɪˈfrɛʃmənts]	點心
expensive	[ɪkˈspɛnsɪv]	昂貴的
late shift		夜班
senior	[ˈsinjɚ]	資深的；最高年級的
gold medal		金牌
in a row		連續
that long		（口語）那麼久

b describing experiences

談過去經驗

真實會話（辦事之前，求取經驗談…）

教授：How's everything, Mike?
（麥可，一切都好吧？）

博士生：Pretty good.
（還很好。）

I am a little worried about defending my thesis this Friday.
（我有點擔心這個星期五的論文口試。）

教授：I am sure you will do fine.
（我肯定你的表現會很好的。）

博士生：What was it like for you?
（你自己作論文口試的時候情況如何呢？）

教授：It was like I was walking with big weights tied to my feet.
（那時好像我腳上綁著兩個重物在走路。）

I felt like I was moving so slow.
（我覺得時間過得好慢。）

博士生：Well, at least you did a good job.
（是嘛，至少你表現得很好啊。）

會話句型進階

It was like I was walking with big weights tied to my feet.
（那好像是在我的腳上綁著重物走路。）

» It was like I had just woken up from a dream.
（那好像是我剛從夢中醒來。）

» It was just like the drive to Shanghai, but longer.
（那就好像開車到上海，只是更久。）

» It was like putting something together without instructions.
（那就好像沒有說明書，要把東西組合起來一樣。）

加強小會話

A It was like I was walking with big weights tied to my feet.
（那就好像我的腳上綁著重物在走路一樣。）

B I hope I don't have that same feeling.
（希望我不會有相同的感覺。）

常用單字成語

defend	[dɪ′fɛnd]	防禦
thesis	[′θisɪs]	論文
(be) like		好像
weight	[wet]	重物
tie to (something)		繫在（某物）
feet		兩腳

slow		慢
at least		至少
felt like		覺得（feel like 的過去式）
dream	[drim]	夢
drive	[draɪv]	開車
feeling	['filɪŋ]	感覺

MP3-49

C imagining what if...

談假設狀況

真實會話（關於尚未發生的事…）

A Have you been following the presidential race?
（你有沒有在注意總統選情？）

B A little.
（有一點。）

Why do you ask?
（你為何有此一問呢？）

A What if Mr. Kim won?
（要是讓金氏贏了呢？）

Can you imagine what it would be like?
（你可以想像那會變成什麼樣子嗎？）

B Not really.
（沒想過。）

A I think we would probably have a better economy.
（我想我們大概經濟會比較好一點。）

B True, but foreign relations would suffer.
（那是實在話，不過外交關係恐怕就會受損。）

會話句型進階

What if Mr. Kim won?
（要是金氏贏了會怎樣呢？）

» What if we had left the house an hour earlier?
（我們要是提早一個鐘頭離開家會怎樣呢？）

» What if Michael was really sick all this time?
（麥克要是這一陣子真的都在生病會怎麼樣呢？）

» What if we won the lottery tomorrow?
（我們要是明天贏了六合彩會怎樣呢？）

加強小會話

A What if Mr. Kim won?
（要是讓金氏贏了會怎樣呢？）

B It is not even possible, so why wonder?
（那是完全不可能的，所以何必操心？）

常用單字成語

what if		要是
won	[wʌn]	贏（win 的過去式）
imagine	[ɪ'mædʒɪn]	想像
economy	[ɪ'kɑnəmɪ]	經濟
foreign relations		對外關係
suffer	['sʌfɚ]	受損
sick		生病
lottery	['lɑtərɪ]	獎券；六合彩
possible	['pɑsəbḷ]	可能的
wonder		猜想

MP3-50

d last year's event
過去式的會話

真實會話（今年與去年的比較…）

A A lot of people showed up tonight!
（今天晚上來的人可真多啊！）

B I know. We hired a lot more people this year.
（我曉得。我們今年增雇了好多人。）

A I also think more people came this year that did not last year.
（其它我還覺得今年來了很多去年沒來的人。）

B Last year's party was really good, though.
（不過，去年的宴會辦得很成功。）

A I am sure this year's will be even better.
（我肯定今年的會比去年好。）

B It is off to a good start!
（那是好的開始。）

會話句型進階

Last year's party was really good, though.
（不過，去年的宴會辦得真是好。）

» Last night's game was great!
（昨天晚上的比賽真是精彩！）

» Last week we had a new couch delivered to my mother.
（上星期我們買了一組新沙發送給我媽媽。）

» Last Thursday I had dinner with the Smiths.
（上星期四我和史密司一家人共進晚餐。）

加強小會話

A Last year's party was really good, though.
（不過，去年的宴會辦得真好。）

B I was not here, so I wouldn't know.
（我沒有來，所以我不知道。）

常用單字成語

show up		出席
hire		雇用
a good start		好的開始
couch	[kaʊtʃ]	沙發椅
deliver	[dɪ'lɪvɚ]	送貨
the Smiths		史密斯一家人

MP3-51

e previous home

新移民會話

真實會話（關懷新移民…）

A How are you getting settled in?
（你安頓的怎麼樣了？）

B Very well, thank you.
（非常好，謝謝你。）

A What is different for you here?
（你認為這裡有什麼相異之處呢？）

B When I was back home, we didn't talk as much with our neighbors.
（在我們家鄉，我們跟鄰居之間沒有講那麼多話。）

A Why is that?
（那是為什麼呢？）

B I don't know.
（我不知道。）

Maybe because we are so crowded, we want all the privacy we can get.
（也許是因為我們那邊人太多了，所以我們要盡可能的有個人穩私。）

會話句型進階

When I was back home, we didn't talk as much with our neighbors.
（在我的家鄉，我們跟鄰居沒有講那麼多的話。）

» When I was in Australia, I went diving on the reefs.
（當我在澳州的時候，我到珊瑚礁去潛水。）

» When Mark was five, he started going to school.
（當馬克五歲的時候，他就開始上學。）

» When we were kids, movies cost a lot less.
（當我們小的時候，電影票便宜很多。）

加強小會話

A When I was back home, we didn't talk as much with our neighbors.
（在我家鄉，我們跟鄰居沒有講那麼多的話。）

B Do you feel like your neighbors are being nosy?
（那你現在覺得你的鄰居好奇心太重了嗎？）

常用單字成語

different	[ˈdɪfərənt]	差異的
as much		一樣多
neighbor	[ˈnebɚ]	鄰居
maybe		也許
crowded	[ˈkraʊdɪd]	擁擠
privacy	[ˈpraɪvəsɪ]	隱私

diving		潛水
reef	[rif]	珊瑚礁
start		開始
nosy	['nozɪ]	好奇

11

talking about future plans

與未來有關的美語

a for kids
談教育

真實會話（關於家庭教師…）

A How is your son doing with school?
（你兒子在學校表現如何？）

B Pretty good. We have hired a tutor to help him.
（非常好。我們請了一位家庭教師來幫助他。）

A Is it helping?
（那有所幫助嗎？）

B I think so.
（我想是吧。）

A We are planning on sending our son to college.
（我們打算讓我兒子去上大學。）

B I would like mine to go also, but he may not be cut out for it.
（我也很想讓我小孩去上大學，不過他可能不是那種料子。）

會話句型進階

We are planning on sending our son to college.
（我們計劃讓我們小孩去上大學。）

» We are planning to leave about three o'clock.
（我們打算大約在三點左右離開。）

» I am planning to run in the Tokyo Marathon.
（我計劃參加東京馬拉松比賽。）

» I am planning to take a week off this summer.
（我打算今年夏天要請一個禮拜的假。）

加強小會話

A We are planning on sending our son to college.
（我們打算讓我們的小孩上大學。）

B I want to send my son to college, too.
（我也要我小孩上大學。）

常用單字成語

son	[sʌn]	兒子
tutor	[ˈtjutɚ]	家庭教師
college	[ˈkɑlɪdʒ]	大學
planning		計畫（plan 的現在分詞）
send		送；遣
mine		我的
cut out for ~		（美語）有～方面的才華
o'clock	[əˈklɑk]	（時間）～點鐘
want to		想要

b after education

談前途規畫

真實會話（學校畢業在即…）

A What are you going to do after you graduate from college?
（你大學畢業以後，打算要做什麼？）

B Later on, I want to work as an electrical engineer.
（將來，我打算要作為一個電機工程師。）

A Wow! What are you doing right now?
（哇！那你現在是做什麼呢？）

B I am working part time for an engineering firm.
（我現在幫一家工程公司打半工。）

A Do you think you will work there after you graduate?
（你認為你畢業以後還會在那裡上班嗎？）

B Yes, if they offer me a full time position.
（是的，只要他們給我全職的職位。）

會話句型進階

Later on, I want to work as an electrical engineer.
（將來，我要作為一個電機工程師。）

» Later on tonight, I want to see a movie.
（今天晚上稍晚，我要去看一部電影。）

» Later on, I hope to be able to run four miles in thirty minutes.
（將來，我希望我能夠在三十分鐘以內跑四英哩。）

» Later on this year, I want to take a vacation to Europe.
（今年稍後，我想到歐洲去度假。）

加強小會話

A Later on, I want to work as an electrical engineer.
（將來，我要作一個電器工程師。）

B It is good to set your goals ahead of time.
（事先訂下你的目標是好的。）

常用單字成語

graduate	[ˈgrædʒʊˌet]	畢業
electrical	[ɪˈlɛktrɪkl̩]	電氣
engineer	[ˌɛndʒəˈnɪr]	工程師
right now		目前
part time		兼職

full time		全職
firm		公司
position		職位
Europe	[ˈjʊrəp]	歐洲
goal		目標
ahead of time		事先

C for work
上班會話

真實會話 （工作很忙…）

A It sure has been a busy month.
（這個月真忙。）

B I know. What are you going to do for next week's shareholder meeting?
（我知道。下星期的股東大會你有什麼要做的？）

A I am going to finish up a slide presentation of this year's profits.
（我必須要完成一份有關今年盈餘的幻燈簡報。）

B I am glad I don't have to present.
（我很高興我不用做簡報。）

A I am sure you will get your turn next year.
（我肯定明年會輪到你。）

B I'll bet you are right.
（我敢打賭你說的一點沒錯。）

會話句型進階

I am going to finish up a slide presentation of this year's profits.
（我必須完成一份有關今年盈餘的幻燈簡報。）

» I am going to build a tree house for my daughter.
（我要幫我女兒在樹上建個小木屋。）

» I am going to write the memo to Mr. Chung this afternoon.
（我今天下午要寫一份給鍾先生的公文。）

» I am going to be in town next week on business.
（我下星期會出差到本市來。）

加強小會話

A I am going to finish up a slide presentation of this year's profits.
（我要完成一份有關今年盈餘的幻燈簡報。）

B Is there anything I can do to help?
（有沒有什麼事是我幫得上忙的呢？）

常用單字成語

next week		下星期
shareholder	[ˈʃɛrˌholdɚ]	股東
meeting		會議
finish up		完成
slide		幻燈片
presentation	[ˌprɛzn̩ˈteʃən]	簡報

profits	[ˈprɑfɪts]	盈餘
(someone's) turn		輪到（某人）
bet		打賭
memo	[ˈmɛmo]	備忘錄；公文
on business		商務的

d for vacation
度假

真實會話（度假時間、地點…）

A I thought you were out of town.
（我以為你到外地了。）

B We are leaving next Friday.
（我們下星期五離開。）

A What are your plans?
（你的計劃是什麼？）

B We are going to fly to the Hawaiian islands.
（我們打算搭機到夏威夷群島。）

A That sounds great!
（聽起來太棒了！）

B I think so.
（我同意。）

My wife and I are both certified divers.
（我和我太太兩個都是有執照的潛水人了。）

會話句型進階

We are going to fly to the Hawaiian islands.
（我們打算搭機到夏威夷群島。）

» We are going to walk to the store.
（我們打算用走的到商店去。）

» We are going to sail to New Zealand next year.
（我們明年要搭船到紐西蘭。）

» We are going to be there for your graduation.
（我們打算去參加你的畢業典禮。）

加強小會話

A We are going to fly to the Hawaiian islands.
（我們打算搭機到夏威夷群島。）

B I've been there twice.
（我曾經去過那裡兩次。）

It is beautiful there.
（那裡好漂亮。）

常用單字成語

out of town		（旅遊；公務）出外
fly	[flaɪ]	搭機旅行
sail		乘船旅行
the Hawaiian islands		夏威夷群島
both		兩者都是

certified	[ˈsɝtɪfaɪd]	有證書的
diver	[ˈdaɪvɚ]	潛水人
New Zealand		（國名）紐西蘭；新西蘭
graduation	[ˌgrædʒʊˈeʃən]	畢業
twice	[twaɪs]	兩次
beautiful	[ˈbjutəfəl]	美麗的

e for tonight
安排事情

真實會話（談下班後的計畫…）

A Are you coming to the company dinner tonight?
（你今天晚上要來參加公司的晚餐嗎？）

B No. I will be driving to Taipei tonight.
（不參加。我今天晚上會開車上台北。）

A Why are you going to Taipei?
（你為什麼要去台北呢？）

B I am going to my brother's wedding.
（我要去參加我哥哥的婚禮。）

A Give him my best wishes.
（請帶給他我衷心的祝福。）

B Thanks. I will.
（謝謝你。我會帶到。）

會話句型進階

I will be driving to Taipei tonight.
（我今天晚上會開車到台北。）

» I will be sleeping in tomorrow!
（我明天要睡得晚一點起床！）

» I'm going to have a good time tonight!
（我今天晚上要玩得很愉快！）

» I will be hungry by the time our food gets here.
（等到我們的餐點上菜我已經餓了。）

加強小會話

A I will be driving to Taipei tonight.
（我今天晚上會開車上台北。）

B Why not take a plane there?
（為什麼不搭機去呢？）

常用單字成語

wedding	[ˈwɛdɪŋ]	婚禮
best		最好的
wish		願望
best wishes		衷心的祝福
hungry	[ˈhʌŋgrɪ]	餓
by the time		到時候
take a plane		搭機

12

getting people to do something
要求別人辦事的美語

MP3-57

a requesting
問路

真實會話（有人在街頭徬徨…）

A Are you all right?
（你還好吧？）

B Yes. I am just a little lost.
（還好。我只是有一點迷了路。）

Could you give me directions to art museum?
（你可以指引我到美術館嗎？）

A Sure. Let me just tell my wife where I am at.
（沒有問題。讓我先告訴我太太我在什麼地方。）

B Don't bother if it will be a problem.
（要是有問題的話，就不用麻煩了。）

A No trouble at all.
（一點都不麻煩。）

I just don't want her to walk off without me.
（我只是不要她一個人走開。）

B Okay. See you in a second.
（好。待會兒再見。）

會話句型進階

Could you give me directions to art museum?
（你能夠指引我到美術館嗎？）

» Could you take a look at this for me?
（你能夠幫我把這個看一看嗎？）

» Could you bring me back a soda?
（你可以幫我帶回一罐汽水嗎？）

» Could you bring me a menu, please?
（可否請你給我一張菜單？）

加強小會話

A Could you give me directions to art museum?
（你可以指引我到美術館嗎？）

B No. I do not know the way, either.
（不行。我自己也不認識路。）

常用單字成語

art		藝術
museum	[mju′ziəm]	博物館
bother	[′bɑðɚ]	麻煩
walk off		離開
second	[′sɛkənd]	（時間）秒
take a look		看看
soda	[′sodə]	汽水
either		也不

MP3-58

b attracting attention

喂！

真實會話（需要別人幫忙…）

A Hey! Would you give me a hand here?
（喂！你能到這兒幫我一個忙嗎？）

B Excuse me?
（你說什麼？）

A Could I get you to come over here for a second?
（我能不能請你到這裡一下？）

B What do you need?
（你有什麼需要嗎？）

A Both my hands are full, and I am about to drop this bag.
（我的兩手都滿滿的，這個袋子快要掉了。）

B Oh, okay, let me grab it for you.
（哦，好啊，讓我幫你拿著。）

會話句型進階

Hey! Would you give me a hand here?
（喂！你能不能到這裡幫我一個忙？）

» Excuse me. Could I get you to help me for a second?
（對不起。可以請你幫我一下忙嗎？）

» Hey! Mark. Is that you?
（喂！馬克。是你嗎？）

» Hey! Did anyone see the car that hit me?
（喂！有沒有人看到撞上我的那部車呀？）

加強小會話

A Hey! Would you give me a hand here?
（喂！你能不能到這兒幫我一個忙？）

B I am sorry, but I am already late.
（很對不起，我在趕時間。）

常用單字成語

give me a hand		幫我忙
excuse	[ɪk'skjuz]	原諒
come over here		過來
full		滿滿的
be about to		即將
drop	[drɑp]	掉下
bag		袋子
hit		撞
already	[ɔl'rɛdɪ]	已經

MP3-59

C help with work

請求協助

真實會話（工作作不完…）

A How are you doing?
（你好嗎？）

B I am swamped!
（我工作太多了！）

A I was pretty busy myself for the last few days.
（過去這幾天，我自己也很忙。）

B Are you still busy?
（你現在還忙嗎？）

A Not really.
（現在不了。）

B Mark has been out sick, so I have gotten behind.
（馬克請病假沒來上班，所以我的進度有點落後。）

I need you to make some calls for me if you have time.
（如果你有時間的話，我需要你幫我打幾通電話。）

會話句型進階

I need you to make some calls for me if you have time.
（如果你有時間的話，我需要你幫我打幾通電話。）

» I need your help with this report.
（我這一份報告需要你幫忙。）

» I need you to write this up when you have time.
（當你有時間的時候，我需要你把這一些寫一寫。）

» I need some help. Are you available?
（我需要幫忙。你有空嗎？）

加強小會話

A I need you to make some calls for me if you have time.
（如果你有時間，我需要你幫我打幾通電話。）

B Sure. I would be glad to help.
（沒問題。我很樂意幫助的。）

常用單字成語

swamped	[swɑmpt]	（美語）工作太多了
last few days		過去幾天
still		仍然
sick		生病
so		所以
get behind		進度落後
have time		有時間
available	[ə'veləbl̩]	有空閒

MP3-60

d help getting somewhere
帶路

真實會話（需要有人送一程…）

A Could I get you to do me a favor?
（我能夠請你幫我一個忙嗎？）

B I will do my best.
（我會盡力而為。）

A I need to get a ride to the airport today after work.
（今天下班，我必須要有人載我去機場。）

B I have to pick my kids up from daycare.
（我必須要到托兒所接我的小孩。）

You might ask John.
（你可能要找約翰。）

A I did. He is busy, too.
（我找過了。他也很忙。）

B Just have one of the secretaries call a cab.
（那就請一位秘書幫你叫一部計程車。）

會話句型進階

Could I get you to do me a favor?
（我可以請你幫我一個忙嗎？）

» Could I get a ride home with you?
（我可以搭你的便車回家嗎？）

» Could I get a ride with you to the company lunch?
（我可以搭你的便車去公司的午餐會嗎？）

» Could you pick up my mail while you are at the box?
（你到郵箱那邊的時候，能不能順便幫我拿我的郵件？）

加強小會話

A Could I get you to do me a favor?
（能請你幫我一個忙嗎？）

B Sure. What do you need?
（當然。你需要什麼呢？）

常用單字成語

favor	[ˈfevɚ]	（美語）幫忙
do me a favor		幫我忙
do my best		盡我可能地
airport	[ˈɛr,port]	機場
after work		下班
daycare	[ˈdeˈkɛr]	（美語）托兒所
secretaries		秘書（secretary 的複數形）
cab		計程車；的士
mail		郵件
box		郵箱

MP3-61

e give opinion

詢問意見

真實會話（需要租車…）

A I need your help, Ms. Lee.
（李小姐，我需要你的幫忙。）

B What can I do for you?
（可以為你做什麼呢？）

A I am looking at rental cars while I am here.
（我在本地的這段時間裡，需要找一部租車。）

Can you tell me which one is the best?
（你可以告訴我那一種車最好嗎？）

B Let's see what you have to choose from.
（我們來看看你有什麼車種可供選擇。）

A Here is the list.
（名單在這裏。）

B I think you will like the Toyota Camry the best.
（我想你會最喜歡豐田的 CAMRY。）

會話句型進階

Can you tell me which one is the best?
（你可以告訴我那一個是最好的嗎？）

» Can you tell me where to go for a romantic dinner?
（你可以告訴我上那兒可以吃一頓浪漫的晚餐嗎？）

» Can you give me some advice on buying a car here?
（你可以給我一些在這裏買車的意見嗎？）

» Can you give me your opinion on this report?
（你可以給我對這份報告的看法嗎？）

加強小會話

A Can you tell me which one is the best?
（你可以告訴我那一樣是最好的嗎？）

B Not really. I do not know enough about it.
（不行，對這個我懂得不夠多。）

常用單字成語

rental	[ˈrɛntḷ]	出租的
rental cars		租車
choose	[tʃuz]	選擇
list		名單
like		喜歡
romantic	[roˈmæntɪk]	浪漫的
opinion	[əˈpɪnjən]	意見

13
talking about something
與事物有關的美語

MP3-62

a cars
購車

真實會話（想買車…）

A Have you seen the new Toyota Corolla?
（你看過新型的豐田 COROLLA 沒有？）

B Yes. It is pretty nice.
（看過，那做得真好。）

A I don't know. It is quite a bit different from the older models.
（我可是不敢說，它跟舊車型比起來有很大不同。）

B How so?
（怎麼會呢？）

A The old Corolla was a plain, basic automobile that was inexpensive and reliable.
（舊款的 COROLLA 是平實基本的汽車，價錢不貴行駛也可靠。）

The new ones have luxury options.
（而新車型卻有奢華的非標準配備以供選擇。）

B The price has not gone up that much though.
（不過價格可沒提高多少啊。）

會話句型進階

It is quite a bit different from the older models.
（它跟舊車型比起來有很大的不同。）

» The new body style is more round than the old.
（新的車身型式比舊型來得圓。）

» Its interior is a lot different than last year's model.
（它的內部與去年的車型比起來有很大的不同。）

» Its engine is the same as the older car's.
（它的引擎跟舊車型是一樣的。）

加強小會話

A I don't know. It is quite a bit different from the older models.
（我可不敢說。它跟舊車型比來有大的不同。）

B I think the changes are for the better.
（我認為這些改變都是朝向好的方向的。）

常用單字成語

quite a bit		很多
older		較舊的
model	[ˈmɑdl̩]	車型，機型
plain		平凡的
basic		基本的
automobile	[ˈɔtəməˌbil]	汽車

inexpensive	[ɪnɪk'spɛnsɪv]	不貴的
reliable	[rɪ'laɪəbl̩]	可靠的
luxury		奢華的
option		非標準配備
go up		上昇
interior	[ɪn'tɪrɪɚ]	內部

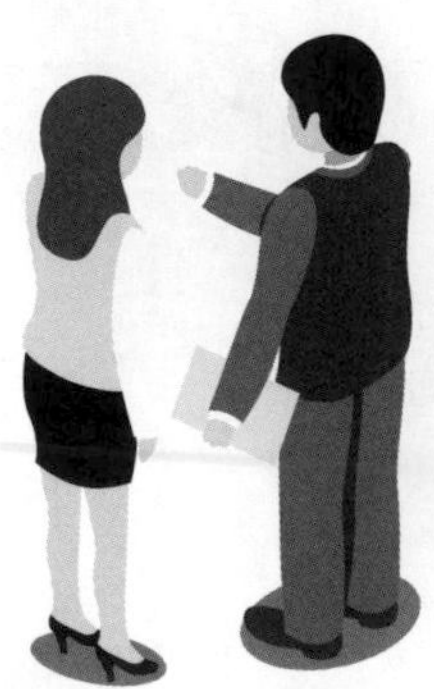

MP3-63

b clothes
購衣服

真實會話（與家人朋友一起購物…）

A Do you think these pants look like the ones I have at home?
（你認為這件褲子跟我家裏那一件很像嗎？）

B The style is the same, but I think these have more pockets.
（樣式相同，不過我認為這些褲子的口袋比較多。）

A I am not sure if I like them.
（我不能肯定我是不是喜歡這些褲子。）

B Are you looking for a change, or do you like the style you wear now?
（你希望尋求改變，還是你喜歡你現在穿的衣服樣式。）

A I want a little change.
（我喜歡有一點改變。）

B Well, try them on and see what you think.
（是嗎，把這些褲子試穿一下，看看你認為如何。）

會話句型進階

The style is the same, but I think these have more pockets.
（樣式是相同，但是我認為這些褲子口袋比較多。）

» The color is the same, but these are more baggy.
（顏色是相同，但這些比較寬鬆。）

» They look the same from here, but you will have to try them on to tell a difference.
（它們看起來是一樣的，不過你必須試穿一下才能看出不同。）

» They are the same brand as your other pair, but the style is different.
（它們跟你另外一雙是同一種品牌，但是樣式有不同。）

加強小會話

A The style is the same, but I think these have more pockets.
（樣式是相同的，不過我認為這些口袋比較多。）

B I do not think that I like them.
（我想我不喜歡它們。）

常用單字成語

at home		在家的
pants	[pænts]	褲子
style		樣式
pocket	[ˈpɑkɪt]	口袋
wear		穿著
try ~ on		試穿～
baggy		寬鬆
tell a difference		分辨差異
brand	[brænd]	品牌

C cities
都市比較

真實會話（與朋友互相談家鄉…）

A Have you been to New York?
（你到過紐約嗎？）

B Yes. I think it is a lot like Taipei.
（到過，我想它非常像台北。）

A Really? Why do you say that?
（真的嗎？你怎麼這麼說呢？）

B They both are crowded cities with a lot of culture.
（它們兩個都市都很擁擠，也很有文化。）

A Taipei is an Asian city and New York is more Western though.
（不過，台北是個亞洲都市，而紐約比較西洋化。）

B That's true, but I was thinking more along the lines of museums and parks.
（那是真的，不過我的想法是針對博物館跟公園這一方面的。）

會話句型進階

I think it is a lot like Taipei.
（我想它非常像台北。）

» I think Beijing is a lot different from Shanghai.
（我認為北京跟上海有非常大的不同。）

» I think that the differences between the two are huge!
（我認為這兩者的相異之處非常巨大。）

» I think that the east coast is very different from the west coast.
（我認為東海岸和西海岸的差異之處非常巨大。）

加強小會話

A I think Tokyo is a lot like Seoul.
（我認為東京非常像漢城。）

B Have you been to both places?
（這兩個地方你都去過嗎？）

常用單字成語

a lot		很多
crowded	[ˈkraʊdɪd]	擁擠的
culture	[ˈkʌltʃɚ]	文化
western		西方的
along the lines of ~		特指～方面而言
park		公園
huge	[hjudʒ]	廣大的
coast		海岸

d movies
討論電影

真實會話 (新電影上片…)

A Did you see the new movie with John Travolta?
(你看過約翰屈伏塔的新電影嗎？)

B Yes, I did.
(是的，我看過了。)

A What did you think of it?
(你認為怎麼樣呢？)

B I really did not like it.
(我真的不喜歡。)

A I thought it was very funny.
(我認為這部電影非常好笑。)

B I just was not in the mood for that kind of humor.
(我沒那個心情去看那種幽默。)

會話句型進階

What did you think of it?
(你認為怎麼樣呢？)

» Did you like the movie?
（你喜歡這部電影嗎？）

» What do you think of the museum exhibit?
（你對博物館的展覽覺得如何？）

» What did you like about the movie?
（你喜歡這部電影的那一點呢？）

加強小會話

A What did you think of it?
（你對它的看法如何呢？）

B I thought it was great.
（我認為它很好。）

I wish I could watch it again!
（我希望我能夠再去看一次。）

常用單字成語

see a movie		看電影
funny	[ˈfʌnɪ]	滑稽
mood		心情
kind		種類
humor	[ˈhjumɚ]	幽默
exhibit	[ɪgˈzɪbɪt]	展覽
great		很好
watch	[wɑtʃ]	觀賞

e vacation resorts
旅遊地點

真實會話（比較旅遊地點…）

A Have you been to the Tahitian islands?
（你到過大溪地群島嗎？）

B Yes, I went ten years ago.
（到過，十年前我去過。）

A How does it compare to Hawaii?
（和夏威夷比較起來如何呢？）

B I don't know how it is now, but when I was there, it was much nicer.
（我不知道大溪地現在變得怎麼樣了，不過我去的時候它是比夏威夷好的多。）

A What was so nice?
（它好在那裏呢？）

B There were no crowds, and not as expensive.
（那裏人少，而且也不那麼貴。）

會話句型進階

I don't know how it is now, but when I was there, it was much nicer.
（我不知道那裏現在怎麼樣，不過當我去的時候，那裏要好得多。）

» I have not been there in a while, but I liked it much better.
（我已好久沒有去了，不過我是比較喜歡它的。）

» It was much nicer than Hawaii.
（它比夏威夷好多了。）

» It was not as developed as Hawaii, but it was nice.
（它的開發不如夏威夷，不過非常好。）

加強小會話

A I don't know how it is now, but when I was there, it was much nicer.
（我不知道那裏現在怎麼樣，不過我去的時候，那裏要好得多。）

B I might call for a brochure.
（我可能會打電話要一份說明書。）

常用單字成語

Tahitian	[tɑ'hɪʃən]	（南太平洋）大溪地的
compare	[kəm'pɛr]	比較
crowd		群眾
as expensive		一樣貴
in a while		一段時間
developed	[dɪ'vɛləpt]	已開發的
call for (something)		打電話去要（某物）
brochure		宣傳小冊

14

express feelings

與情緒有關的美語

MP3-67

a complaining

抱怨

真實會話（同事原本說要看電影…）

A Did you get to go to the movies last night?
（你昨天晚上去看電影了嗎？）

B No. I had the most horrible night.
（沒有，我度過了一個最糟糕的夜晚。）

A Why is that?
（怎麼說呢？）

B I got home and the house was a mess, and then I spilled tea on my shirt right before leaving.
（我回到家時，家裏亂七八糟，然後就在我要出門時，我打翻了一杯茶倒在我的襯衫上。）

A I am sorry to hear that.
（真遺憾聽到這樣。）

B We are going to try to go this weekend.
（我們打算這個週末再去看看。）

會話句型進階

I had the most horrible night.
（我渡過了最糟糕的夜晚。）

» I had the worst service at that restaurant.
（我在那家餐館獲得最糟糕的服務。）

» I don't like anything on the menu!
（菜單上的所有東西我都不喜歡。）

» I can't find anything to get rid of this headache!
（我找不到東西可以消除這個頭疼。）

加強小會話

A I had the most horrible night.
（我渡過一個最糟糕的夜晚。）

B I am sorry to hear it.
（很遺憾聽你這樣說。）

Mine was not too great, either.
（我的也不怎麼好。）

常用單字成語

horrible	[ˈhɔrəbl̩]	糟糕的
mess	[mɛs]	一團糟
spill		打翻
shirt		襯衫
weekend	[ˈwikˈɛnd]	週末
worst		最壞的
service		服務
get rid of		消除
headache	[ˈhɛdˌek]	頭痛

MP3-68

b apologizing
道歉

真實會話（覺得朋友的衣著不好看…）

A That shirt does not look very good on you.
（那件襯衫穿在你身上不怎麼好看。）

B That was rude!
（那樣說太魯莽。）

A I'm sorry.
（對不起。）

I did not mean to hurt your feelings.
（我不是有意去傷你的心。）

B That's okay.
（算了。）

I don't like the shirt, either.
（我自己也不喜歡。）

A Why do you wear it?
（那你為什麼穿著呢？）

B My wife bought it for me.
（因為是我太太買給我。）

會話句型進階

I'm sorry. I did not mean to hurt your feelings.
（對不起，我不是有意要傷你的心。）

» I apologize if I hurt your feelings.
（如果有傷到你的感情，我道歉。）

» I am really sorry. What can I do to make it up to you?
（我真的很抱歉，我應該要怎麼樣做才能補償你呢？）

» Please accept my apology.
（請接受我的道歉。）

加強小會話

A I'm sorry, I did not mean to hurt your feelings.
（很對不起，我不是有意要傷你的心的。）

B What did you expect！
（你要我怎麼樣嘛！）

常用單字成語

look good		看起來好看
rude	[rud]	魯莽的
mean to		有意要……
hurt		傷害
feelings	[ˈfilɪŋz]	人的感情
bought		買（buy 的複數）

apologize	[ə'pɑlə,dʒaɪz]	道歉
make it up		補償
accept	[ək'sɛpt]	接受
apology	[ə'pɑlədʒɪ]	道歉
expect	[ɪk'spɛkt]	期待

C forgiving
不計較

真實會話（無意間透露朋友的秘密…）

A I hope I did not offend you by talking about you to John.
（我希望我對約翰談到你，不會冒犯你。）

B I was a little hurt.
（那對我是有一點不好。）

A I apologize.
（我道歉。）

I did not know that I was the only one you talked to about quitting.
（我不知道你把要辭職的事僅僅告訴我一個人。）

B It's okay.
（沒有關係。）

Thanks for your apology.
（謝謝你的道歉。）

A I will make sure John keeps it to himself.
（我會確保約翰保守這個秘密。）

B I already talked to him.
（我已經跟他講過了。）

會話句型進階

It's okay. Thanks for your apology.
（沒有關係，謝謝你的道歉。）

» I understand Thanks anyway.
（我了解，還很謝謝你。）

» Don't think any more of it.
（不要再去想它了。）

» I forgive you, just don't do it again.
（我原諒你，只是以後不要再犯了。）

加強小會話

A It's okay. Thanks for your apology.
（沒有關係，謝謝你的道歉。）

B If there is anything I can do, let me know.
（如果有什麼事是我可以做的，讓我知道。）

常用單字成語

offend	[ə'fɛnd]	冒犯
talk about ~		談論關於～的事
quitting		辭職（quit 的動名詞）
make sure		確保
keeps it to (oneself)		（某人）保守秘密
understand	[ˌʌndɚ'stænd]	理解
anyway		無論如何還是……
forgive	[fɚ'gɪv]	原諒

d disappointment
失望與沮喪

真實會話（同事不能調職國外…）

A I heard you are not going to be able to go work in Holland.
（我聽說你不能到荷蘭去工作了。）

B Yes, they gave the assignment to Janny Huang instead.
（是的，他們把那份差事指派給黃珍妮了。）

A What do you think about it?
（那你有什麼看法呢？）

B I am just a little bummed out.
（我感到有一點失望。）

A I would be, too.
（如果是我我也會。）

I wonder why they changed their minds.
（我在想，為什麼他們會改變主意？）

B Janny is not married.
（珍妮沒結婚。）

The company felt it was too expensive to move my family there.
（公司認為把我全家搬遷到那裏開銷太大。）

會話句型進階

I am just a little bummed out.
（我只是有一些失望。）

» I am a little disappointed, but I will get over it.
（我有一些失望，不過我會恢復的。）

» I was really looking forward to going.
（我真的很想去的。）

» I am pretty sad about not going.
（不能去讓我感到很傷心。）

加強小會話

A I am just a little bummed out.
（我只是有一些失望。）

B If I can cheer you up, let me know.
（如果我能夠鼓舞你的精神，請讓我知道。）

常用單字成語

assignment	[ə'saɪnmənt]	工作機會；任務
instead	[ɪn'stɛd]	反而
bum		（美語）掃興
bummed out		（美語）太失望了
changed (one's) mind		（某人）改變主意
move		搬遷
disappointed	[dɪsə'pɔɪntɪd]	失望的
get over		恢復
look forward to		渴望
sad		非常失望；悲傷
cheer	[tʃɪr]	（鼓勵）加油

MP3-71

e happiness/excitement
快樂

真實會話（心裡很高興…）

A Did you hear the good news?
（你聽到那個好消息了嗎？）

B No, what's going on?
（沒有，怎麼了？）

A I am so excited.
（我非常興奮。）

I get to go to Hawaii for vacation!
（我可以去夏威夷渡假。）

B That's great.
（那太好了。）

When do you go?
（你幾時去呀？）

A I leave next Friday.
（我下星期五走。）

B Well, take lots of pictures!
（是嗎？要拍很多照片哦。）

會話句型進階

I am so excited. I get to go to Hawaii for vacation!
（我非常興奮我可以去夏威夷渡假。）

» I am so happy that I get to see the exhibit.
（很高興我可以看這個展覽。）

» I am so excited about the game tonight!
（對於今天晚上的比賽我感到很興奮。）

» I am really happy to hear about your grandson's graduation.
（聽說你孫兒畢業，我感到很高興。）

加強小會話

A I am so excited. I get to go to Hawaii for vacation!
（我太興奮了，我可以到夏威夷去渡假。）

B I wish I could go with you!
（我真希望我可以跟你一道去。）

常用單字成語

get to (do)	得以（做某事）
excited	興奮的
for vacation	渡假
picture	照片；圖片
take pictures	拍照片
grandson	孫子
wish	但願

15

dealing with moods and feelings

表達感覺的美語

MP3-72

a anger
生氣

真實會話（非常不滿會議的決定⋯）

A Can you believe that meeting today?
（今天的會議竟會那樣，真不敢相信！）

B I know. That new deadline is impossible.
（我曉得你的意思，新訂出來的截止日期根本是不可能達成的。）

A I am so mad that I could explode.
（我氣得都要爆炸了。）

B Me, too.
（我也是。）

But we have to focus on that new deadline.
（不過我們得專注在那個新的截止日期上。）

A I know. I just need a few minutes to calm down.
（我知道。我只是須要幾分鐘冷靜下來。）

B OK. Meet me in my office later.
（好的，稍後到我的辦公室來見我吧。）

會話句型進階

I am so mad that I could explode.
（我好生氣，幾乎要爆炸了。）

» I am so upset. I need to calm down.
（我很生氣，我必須要冷靜下來。）

» I haven't been this angry in years.
（我有好多年沒這樣生氣了。）

» I'm too mad to deal with that problem now.
（我太生氣了，現在沒辦法處理那個問題。）

加強小會話

A I am so mad that I could explode.
（我氣得幾乎要爆炸了。）

B I'm mad, too.
（我也很生氣。）
But we have to finish this project.
（不過我還是得把這個專案做完。）

常用單字成語

deadline	截止時間
impossible	不可能的
explode	爆炸
have to	必須
focus on	專心於
calm down	冷靜下來
upset	生氣
in years	好多年
mad	（美語）生氣

b sadness
憂鬱

真實會話（對方情緒低落…）

M Hey Sally, are you OK?
（喂，莎莉你還好嗎？）

W I'm fine, just a little down.
（我還好，只是有一些提不起精神。）

M Is there anything that I can do?
（我可以幫上什麼忙嗎？）

W No, thanks for offering.
（不，謝謝你的好意。）

I just miss my husband.
（我只是思念我先生。）

M Where did he go?
（他去那裏呢？）

W He's away on work and won't be back for two more weeks.
（他出差了，要再兩個禮拜才會回來。）

會話句型進階

I'm fine, just a little down.
（我很好，只是有些意興闌珊。）

» I feel a little blue today.
（我今天覺得有些憂鬱。）

» This day is really bringing me down.
（今天真是讓我提不起精神。）

» I wish I could get over these blues.
（真希望我能克服這些憂鬱。）

加強小會話

A I'm fine, just a little down.
（我還好，只是有點意興闌珊。）

B Sorry to hear that.
（聽到你這樣真是遺憾。）

Anything I can do?
（我可以幫忙嗎？）

常用單字成語

fine		（情況）好的
a little down		（美語）有些消沈
miss		懷念
husband	[ˈhʌzbənd]	丈夫
away		離開
blue		（美語）憂鬱

MP3-74

C indifference
漠不關心

真實會話（同事中有人升遷…）

A Hi Jack, did you hear the news?
（嗨傑克，你聽到消息了嗎？）

B No, what?
（沒有，什麼消息？）

A Bob got the promotion to sales manager.
（鮑伯升業務經理了。）

B Oh, OK.
（哦，是嗎？）

A So what do you think?
（那你有什麼看法呢？）

B I could really care less.
（我才不管那麼多呢？）

會話句型進階

I could really care less.
（我才不管那麼多呢。）

» It really doesn't matter to me.
（那與我絲毫無關。）

» Why should I care?
（我為什麼要關心？）

» Hey, whatever you say.
（好吧，隨你怎麼說了。）

加強小會話

A I could really care less.
（我才不管那稽ｈ呢。）

B OK, I just thought I'd let you know.
（算了，我只是想應該讓你曉得。）

常用單字成語

promotion	[prə'moʃən]	擢昇
sales		銷售
manager	['mænədʒɚ]	經理
less		更少
care less		（美語）漠不關心
whatever		無論什麼

d concern

擔心

真實會話（朋友出了交通事故…）

A I heard about your accident this weekend.
（我聽説你這個周末出了交通事故。）

Are you OK?
（你還好嗎？）

B I'm fine, but my car sure isn't.
（我還好，不過我的車就不好了。）

A If you need a ride to work, just let me know.
（如果你必須要搭便車上班，讓我知道。）

B Thanks for the offer, but I live within walking distance.
（謝謝你的好意，不過我住在走路就可到的地方。）

A Well, if you need a ride to the store or anything, just call.
（是嗎，如果你需要搭車去商店購物，或做其他的事，就打電話給我。）

B Thanks. I will keep that in mind.
（謝謝你，我會記在心上的。）

會話句型進階

Are you OK?
（你還好嗎？）

» Is there anything I can do for you?
（有我需要幫忙的嗎？）

» How are you doing?
（你一切都好嗎？）

» Can I help you in any way?
（有什麼可以幫得上忙的嗎？）

加強小會話

A Are you OK?
（你還好嗎？）

B I'm fine. Thanks for asking.
（我還好，謝謝你的關心。）

常用單字成語

accident	[ˈæksədənt]	交通事故
distance	[ˈdɪstəns]	距離
walking distance		走路可到的路程
keep in mind		記著
in any way		在任何方面

MP3-76

e happiness
快樂

真實會話（對方很快樂的樣子…）

A Boy, you're glowing today.
（唉呀，你今天真是容光煥發。）

What's up?
（有什麼事嗎？）

B My boyfriend proposed to me this weekend!
（我男朋友上周末跟我求婚。）

A Congratulations.
（恭喜你了。）

B Thanks, I have never been so happy.
（謝謝，我從來沒有這樣快樂過。）

A So when is the big day?
（那麼大喜之日是那一天呢？）

B I don't know yet.
（我還不知道。）

We are still discussing it.
（我們仍然在討論之中。）

會話句型進階

I have never been so happy.
（我從來沒有這樣快樂過。）

» This is the best day of my life.
（這是我這輩子最美好的一天。）

» That news made my day.
（那一個消息讓我樂不可支。）

» Things just can't get any better.
（不可能再有比這美好的事。）

加強小會話

A I have never been so happy.
（我從來沒有這樣快樂過。）

B That's great.
（那太好了。）

I am happy for you.
（我為你感到高興。）

常用單字成語

boy		（美語感嘆詞）哎呀
glowing	[ˈgloɪŋ]	亮麗
boyfriend		男朋友
propose	[prəˈpoz]	求婚
congratulations	[kənˌgrætʃəˈleʃənz]	恭喜
discuss		討論

16
During Conversation
會話中的美語

MP3-77

a hesitating

事情尚未決定

真實會話（有事等著做最後決定…）

A So are you going to buy the new computer system for the clerical staff?
（那你打算要給辦事職員買新的電腦了嗎？）

B Well, that is still on the table.
（這個，那件事還沒決定呢。）

A When will you know?
（你幾時會知道呢？）

B Our next meeting is two weeks from today.
（從今天算起兩個星期我們還要開個會。）

We'll see then.
（到時候再看吧。）

A What do you think the verdict will be?
（你認為決定會是如何呢？）

B We'll just have to wait and see.
（我們只能等著瞧。）

會話句型進階

Well, that is still on the table.
（這個嘛，那件事還沒決定呢。）

» That proposal is at the top of my list.
（那個企畫案在我的工作表上，是最上面的一件。）

» I need another week to look over that.
（我需要再一個星期的時間整個重覆再看一下。）

» Let me get back to you on that to iron out the details.
（關於那件事讓我再跟你連絡來決定一下細節。）

加強小會話

A Well, that is still on the table.
（這個嘛，整個事情還沒決定呢。）

B When will you have a definite answer?
（何時會有肯定的答案呢？）

常用單字成語

system	[ˈsɪstəm]	系統
clerical	[ˈklɛrɪkl̩]	辦事員的
staff		部屬；人員
still on the table		仍未決定
verdict	[ˈvɝdɪkt]	判決；決議
wait and see		等著瞧
proposal	[prəˈpozl̩]	企畫
look over		複查文件
iron out		做出
detail		細節
definite	[ˈdɛfənɪt]	確定的

MP3-78

b interrupting politely
讓我打岔一下

真實會話（開會中，需要打岔…）

A Excuse me, sorry to interrupt.
（對不起，抱歉要打岔一下。）

B Yes, what can I do for you?
（沒問題，有什麼事要我做呢？）

A Your wife is on line one.
（你太太在一線電話。）

B Tell her I'm in a meeting and will call back.
（告訴他我在開會，我會給她回電話。）

A She said it was an emergency.
（她說是緊急事件。）

That is why I interrupted.
（我才打岔。）

B Oh, thank you.
（哦，謝謝你。）

會話句型進階

Excuse me, sorry to interrupt.
（對不起，抱歉要打岔一下。）

» Pardon me, can I ask you a quick question.
（對不起，我可以很快的問你一個問題嗎？）

» Please excuse my interruption, I need you to sign this.
（請原諒我打岔，我需要你在這裏簽名。）

» Sorry to interrupt, I need to talk to you.
（對不起要打個岔，我需要跟你談一談。）

加強小會話

A Excuse me, sorry to interrupt.
（對不起，很抱歉要打岔。）

B That's OK.
（沒有關係。）

What do you need?
（你需要什麼嗎？）

常用單字成語

interrupt	[ɪntə'rʌpt]	打岔
emergency	[ɪ'mɝdʒənsɪ]	緊急
on line one		（電話）在第一線
call back		回電話
pardon	['pɑrdən]	原諒
quick		快的
interruption		打岔
sign		簽名

MP3-79

C bringing in other people politely

你的看法如何？

真實會話（詢問有經驗者的看法…）

A I think Robert's proposal is a tremendous idea.
（我認為羅伯的建議真是個好主意。）

What's your view on this, Jackie?
（潔姬，你對這件事的看法如何？）

B It sounds interesting.
（那個企畫聽起來很有趣。）

A I know you've worked in this area before.
（我知道在這方面你從前做過。）

B Thanks for asking.
（謝謝你問我的意見。）

In my opinion this plan is good.
（按照我的意見這個計劃是好的。）

A It sounds like a good idea then.
（那麼整個聽起來就是個好主意啦。）

會話句型進階

What's your view on this, Jackie?
（潔姬，對這件事你的看法如何？）

» How do you feel about this, Adam?
（亞當，對這件事你覺得如何？）

» I'd love to hear your opinion on this topic.
（在這件主題上，我很想聽你的意見。）

» What do you think about this, Sally?
（莎莉，關於這件事你的想法如何？）

加強小會話

A What's your view on this, Jackie?
（潔姬，關於這件事你的觀點如何？）

B I don't know much about this subject.
（在這個課題上我知道得不多。）

常用單字成語

tremendous	[trɪ'mɛndəs]	巨大的；很好的
interesting	[ɪn'trɪstɪŋ]	有趣的
in my opinion		根據我的看法
topic		主題
subject		主題

MP3-80

d having to leave

我得走了！

真實會話（時間很晚了…）

A Is it already ten o'clock?
（已經十點了。）

B I know!
（我知道。）

Hasn't the night flown by.
（時間過得好快哦。）

A I hate to run out like this, but I have to leave.
（我實在不喜歡就這樣離開，不過我得走了。）

B Is everything OK?
（沒什麼要緊的事吧？）

A Yes, my sitter has to be home by eleven.
（是的，我請的保姆必須要在十一點以前回家。）

B I understand.
（我了解。）

My kids are at my parents' tonight.
（我的小孩今天晚上都在我父母那裏。）

會話句型進階

I hate to run out like this, but I have to leave.
（我很不喜歡就這樣離開，不過我得走了。）

» Sorry, but I have to be somewhere.
（對不起，我得到別地方去。）

» Thanks for everything. I have to run.
（謝謝你的一切招待，我得走了。）

» The dinner was great, but I have to go.
（這頓晚餐真是豐盛，可是我得走了。）

加強小會話

A I hate to run out like this, but I have to leave.
（我不喜歡就這樣離開，可是我必須要走。）

B Well, thanks for stopping by.
（是嗎，謝謝你來拜訪。）

常用單字成語

flown	[flon]	飛（fly 的過去分詞）
fly by		（時間）飛逝
hate		恨
sitter		保姆（baby-sitter 的簡稱）
stop by		順道拜訪

MP3-81

e changing topic
如何改變話題

真實會話（對話題沒興趣…）

A Did you hear about Jack and Mary?
（你聽說傑克和瑪麗的事沒有？）

B No, but have you seen the movie Star Wars?
（沒有。哎！你看過電影星際大戰沒有？）

A No, I haven't.
（沒有，我還沒去看。）

B You really need to see it.
（你應該要去看。）

A I'm not a big sci-fi fan.
（我不是個很大的科幻電影迷。）

B This one you will like.
（這部電影你會喜歡的。）

It is a really good movie.
（它真是一部好電影。）

會話句型進階

No, but have you seen the movie Star Wars?
（沒有。哎！你看過星際大戰這部電影沒有。）

» Interesting, did you see the baseball game last night?
（你講的有意思。對了，你昨天晚上有沒有看棒球賽？）

» Really, are you going to the party tomorrow?
（真的這樣啊，你明天要去參加宴會嗎？）

» Oh yeah. Hey, did you catch the Giant game?
（是嗎？哎！你有沒有看巨人的那一場比賽？）

加強小會話

A No, but have you seen the movie Star Wars?
（沒有。哎！你有沒有看過星際大戰這部電影？）

B No. Do you recommend it?
（不，你推薦我去看嗎？）

常用單字成語

sci-fi		科幻
fan		（電影、運動等）迷
baseball	[ˈbesbɔl]	棒球
catch	[kætʃ]	趕上
recommend		推薦

17

Making suggestions and giving advice

提意見的美語

MP3-82

a about where to eat

你有什麼建議？

真實會話（對方問你夜間計畫…）

A What are you and Jane doing tonight?
（你和珍妮今天晚上要做什麼？）

B I think we'll just grab a bite to eat and call it a night.
（我想我們只會隨便買個東西吃，然後就睡覺了。）

A You guys should try the new Korean restaurant downtown.
（你們兩位應該去試試市區裡新開的那一家韓國餐館。）

B Really, what do you suggest?
（真的，你建議我們吃什麼？）

A Try spicy noodles.
（試試辣麵。）

They are great.
（那一家辣麵做得很好。）

B Thanks for the tip.
（謝謝你提供我這個消息。）

會話句型進階

You guys should try the new Korean restaurant downtown.
（你們應該試試市區新開的那一家韓國餐館。）

» You have to try the sushi bar next door.
（你應該去試試隔壁的壽司台。）

» We have to eat Italian at the Olive restaurant.
（我們可得去橄欖餐廳吃意大利菜。）

» You should try John's pizzeria for pizza.
（你們應該試試約翰比薩店的比薩。）

加強小會話

A You guys should try the new Korean restaurant downtown.
（你們應該試試市區那一家新開的韓國餐館。）

B Hey, thanks for the suggestion.
（喂，謝謝你的建議。）

常用單字成語

call it a night		今晚不再繼續
guys		（美語）你們
Korean	[kə'riən]	韓國的
spicy	['spaɪsɪ]	辣
noodle		麵
tlp		秘訣
sushi		（日本食物）壽司
pizzeria	[ˌpitsə'riə]	披薩店
pizza		披薩餅

MP3-83

b sights to see

有什麼好觀光的？

真實會話（打聽度假地點…）

A I can't wait for my vacation.
（我等不及我的假期了。）

B Really, where are you going?
（真的啊，你們打算要到那裏去？）

A We are going to New Orleans.
（我們要去紐奧爾良。）

B You have to go see the garden district.
（你們必須要去看花園區。）

A I've heard about it.
（我聽説那個地方。）

What's there?
（那裡有什麼呢？）

B These great old houses surrounded by huge oak trees.
（有許多巨大的舊房子，四周都是巨大的橡樹圍繞著。）

會話句型進階

You have to go see the garden district.
（你們必須要去看花園區。）

» You have to go to the museum.
（你必須要去博物館。）

» You should stop by the aquarium if you get a chance.
（如果你有機會的話，必須要去看看水族館。）

» Make sure you walk around the downtown area.
（你務必要用走路的，逛逛市中心區域。）

加強小會話

A You have to go see the garden district.
（你必須要去看花園區。）

B My wife has really wanted to see that place.
（我太太真的很想去看那個地方。）

常用單字成語

garden	[ˈgɑrdən]	花園
district	[ˈdɪstrɪkt]	區域
surround	[səˈraʊnd]	環繞
oak		橡樹
aquarium	[əˈkwɛrɪəm]	水族館

C about children

電話幾號？

真實會話（問電話號碼…）

A You look tired. Are you OK?
（你看起來好累，你還好嗎？）

B I'm fine.
（我還好。）

My little daughter was up with an earache last night.
（我女兒昨天晚上一夜沒睡，耳朵疼。）

A You have to take her to my pediatrician.
（你得要帶她去看我的小兒科醫生。）

B Who is he?
（他是誰呀？）

A Dr. Stone. He is absolutely wonderful.
（史東醫生，他絕對是非常好的。）

B Great. What is the number?
（太好了，電話號碼是幾號？）

會話句型進階

You have to take her to my pediatrician.
（你得帶她去看我的小兒科醫生。）

- You should call my sitter. She's great.
（你應該打電話找我的保母，她非常好的。）
- My kids love the new pizza place. You should try it.
（我的小孩很喜歡新開比薩店，你們應該去試試。）
- You should take your kids to see The Lion King.
（你應該帶你們的小孩去看獅子王。）

加強小會話

A You have to take her to my pediatrician.
（你得帶她去看我的小兒科醫生。）

B We have one of our own, but thanks.
（我們自己有小兒科醫生，謝謝你。）

常用單字成語

earache	[ˈɪrˌek]	耳朵痛
pediatrician	[ˌpidɪəˈtrɪʃən]	小兒科醫生
absolutely	[ˈæbsəlutlɪ]	絕對地
wonderful	[ˈwʌndɚfəl]	好極了
number		號碼

MP3-85

d about cars

我筋疲力盡了！

真實會話（買車…）

A Boy, am I exhausted!
（唉呀，我真的是精疲力盡。）

B Why, what did you do this weekend?
（為什麼呢，這個周末你都做什麼事呢？）

A I looked at cars all weekend.
（我整個周末都去看車。）

B You should really take a look at the Toyota Camry.
（你真的需要去看一下豐田的 CAMRY。）

A Is that what you drive?
（你開的就是那一型的車嗎？）

B No, but I would if I was buying a new car.
（不，不過我如果要買新車的話，會買那一型。）

會話句型進階

You should really take a look at the Toyota Camry.
（你真的應該去看一下豐田的的 CAMRY。）

» You should get your tires at Goodyear.
（你應該到「固特異」去換你的車胎。）

» You should have your oil changed at Kwik Lube. They do good work.
（你應該到「快客」機油行去換機油，他們的工作做得很好。）

» Before committing to a new car, read consumer reports.
（在你下定決心買新車之前先讀讀消費者報告。）

加強小會話

A You should really take a look at the Toyota Camry.
（你真的應該看一下豐田的的 CAMRY。）

B I'm looking for a sports car.
（我在找的是跑車。）

常用單字成語

exhausted	[ɪgˈzɔstɪd]	筋疲力盡
tire		車胎
oil		（汽車、機車）機油
commit	[kəˈmɪt]	承諾
consumer	[kənˈsumɚ]	消費者
sports car		（車型）跑車

e about co-worker

你怎麼了？

真實會話（對方不高興…）

A You seem unhappy.
（你似乎不高興。）

What's up?
（怎麼了？）

B Nothing. I feel like Jack doesn't listen to my ideas.
（沒什麼，我覺得好像傑克都不聽我的想法。）

A Oh, don't let him get you down.
（哦，不要讓他使你情緒不好。）

He's just hard to work with.
（那個人是不容易一起工作的。）

B Well, I don't know what to do anymore.
（是啊，我都不知道要怎麼做了。）

A Just keep up the good work and ignore his moods.
（你只管把工作做好，不要去理他的心情。）

B I'll try.
（我會試著這樣的。）

I just wish we got along better.
（我只是希望我們能夠相處愉快一點。）

會話句型進階

Just keep up the good work and ignore his moods.
（只管把工作做好，不要去理他的心情。）

» Don't worry about Sally. Worry about your work.
（不要為莎莉擔心，要掛念你的工作。）

» Don't get involved in your workers' problems.
（不要牽扯進你同事的問題。）

» Try not to get upset over small things she says.
（試著不要因為他所說的一些小事情而生氣。）

加強小會話

A Just keep up the good work and ignore his moods.
（只管把工作做好，不要去理他的心情。）

B Thanks, I just get frustrated.
（謝謝你，我只不過覺得挫折感很重。）

常用單字成語

unhappy		不高興
listen		聽
hard		困難
ignore	[ɪg′nɔr]	不理
moods		情緒
got along		想處
involve	[ɪn′vɑlv]	介入
get upset		（美語）生氣

好流利! 用英語聊不停

英語系列：52

作者／施孝昌
出版者／哈福企業有限公司
地址／新北市板橋區五權街16號
電話／(02) 2808-6545　傳真／(02) 2808-6545
郵政劃撥／31598840　戶名／哈福企業有限公司
出版日期／2018年11月　再版二刷／2018年12月
定價／NT$ 299元 (附MP3)

全球華文國際市場總代理／采舍國際有限公司
地址／新北市中和區中山路2段366巷10號3樓
電話／(02) 8245-8786　傳真／(02) 8245-8718
網址／www.silkbook.com 新絲路華文網

香港澳門總經銷／和平圖書有限公司
地址／香港柴灣嘉業街12號百樂門大廈17樓
電話／(852) 2804-6687　傳真／(852) 2804-6409
定價／港幣100元 (附MP3)

email／haanet68@Gmail.com
網址／Haa-net.com
facebook／Haa-net 哈福網路商城

國家圖書館出版品預行編目資料

好流利!用英語聊不停 / 施孝昌著. -- 新北市：哈福企業, 2018.11
面；　公分. -- (英語系列；52)

ISBN 978-986-96282-7-3(平裝附光碟片)

1.英語 2.會話

805.165　　107019350

哈福

哈福